Scones,  Skulls & Scams

Leighann Dobbs

This is a work of fiction.

None of it is real. All names, places, and events are products of the author's imagination. Any resemblance to real names, places, or events are purely coincidental, and should not be construed as being real.

Chapter One

Lexy Baker-Perillo stared lazily out the floor-to-ceiling window that made up the front wall of her bakery, *The Cup and Cake*. A sigh escaped her lips as she watched the last leaf drop from the century's old oak tree on the riverbank and float lazily toward the falls, picking up speed until it catapulted over the edge.

Fall was nearing an end. The trees were bare and the air had a chill—a sharp contrast to the palm tree filled Tropical Island where she'd just spent two weeks honeymooning with her hunky homicide detective husband, Jack Perillo.

The honeymoon had been wonderfully romantic and restful, but Lexy was happy to be back home and back into baking and running her business.

Turning, she inspected the front room of the bakery. The glass cases displaying her baked goods gleamed in the sunlight. The self-serve coffee station filled the room with the rich aroma of dark roast. The cafe tables, set up next to the window overlooking the scenic waterfall that gave the town of Brook Ridge Falls its name, were spotlessly clean ... and empty.

While honeymooning, she'd left the running of her bakery in the care of her assistant and best friend, Cassie. Lexy felt a swell of pride her friend had handled everything perfectly with no problems at all.

Well, almost perfectly ... sales had dropped off considerably in her absence, but it didn't have anything to do with Cassie running the shop. Lexy turned back to look out the window. She knew the reason sales had fallen off—she was staring straight at it.

"It" was the new bakery across the street, which had sprung into business while Lexy had been on her honeymoon. When she'd left, the windows in the new bakery had been covered in brown craft paper. A small handwritten sign in the corner had been the only indication a bakery might take up residence. Today, that bakery appeared to be fully stocked and a line of customers filed out the door and into the street.

Surely her baked goods can't be that *delicious —could they?*

More than likely, the big turnout had more to do with the fifty-percent-off sign in the shop window and the fact the sidewalk leading up to Lexy's bakery had been dug up because of the new sewer lines they were installing. On the other side of the street, the sidewalk leading up to the *other* bakery were perfectly fine.

Lexy squinted over at the store trying to see inside. It looked to be set up almost identical to *The Cup and Cake,* with glass displays, cafe tables, and a self-serve coffee station. She'd even chosen a name similar to Lexy's—*The Brew and Bake*—and had the sign made in the same shape and pink color as Lexy's sign.

Lexy started as a familiar figure appeared in the door of *The Brew and Bake.*

That couldn't be who she thought it was ... could it?

Lexy sucked in a breath as the door opened to reveal her grandmother Mona Baker, or Nans as Lexy called her, and Nans' three closest friends—Ida, Helen and Ruth. Lexy noticed with dismay that, not only had the traitorous senior citizens been inside the bakery, they were also carrying bakery bags that looked to be loaded with pastries!

Her hands curled into tight fists as she watched them walk across the street, giggling and looking inside each other's bags.

Surely, they weren't bringing pastries from the *other* bakery over to her shop?

But they were.

Lexy stood, whirling around to face the door as the four women came in.

"Just what do you think you're doing?" Lexy demanded.

The women's happy chatter stopped abruptly. They stared at her with puzzled looks.

"Don't get upset dear. We're just going to compare the *inferior* goods from the other bakery to yours," Nans said as if Lexy should have known that's what they were doing.

"Oh." Lexy felt mollified since Nans had referred to the other bakery's pastries as inferior. She relaxed her stance and unclenched her fists. "Why?"

"We're going to do a taste test and Helen is going to take notes, then write up an article for the *Brook Ridge Sentinel* detailing the results and how your baked goods taste much better," Nans answered.

"Provided they *are* better, of course," Ruth added then grimaced as Nans elbowed her in the ribs. "I mean, we know they're better, of course. We just need to prove it."

"Right, so let's get some of the same types of pastries for the taste test." Ida rubbed her hands together and made a beeline for the display cases.

The women rummaged through their bags looking at the items they'd purchased—lemon bars, brownies, éclairs, pound cake, blueberry muffins and cupcakes. They picked out identical items from Lexy's display case and took them to a table, where they spread out some napkins on which they lined up the baked goods.

"Now these are from Lexy." Ruth pointed to the row on the top, "And these are from that other place." The way she said the words *that other place,* with a hint of disgust made Lexy smile as she pulled a chair up to join the older ladies.

Nans handed out the plates and forks she'd grabbed from the self-serve station. "We'll each take a bite from each one and then discuss the differences like they do on those cooking shows on TV."

Helen pulled open her gigantic beige patent leather purse and rummaged around inside it pulling out various items—a lipstick, tissues, duct tape—until finally producing an iPad, which she plopped on the table in front of her.

"Okay, I'm ready," she said as she reached across the table, her fork slicing off a corner of the brownie from *The Brew and Bake.*

Lexy held her breath as Helen brought the fork to her mouth. She made exaggerated chewing motions, moving her tongue around in her mouth and licking her lips. Then she wrinkled up her nose and made a big show of swallowing.

"Tastes stale." She sat back and typed something into the iPad.

Lexy let out her breath. The others reached over with their forks taking little pieces of the pastries and putting them on their plates.

"Now let's not mix up which pastry is from which bakery," Nans said as she bit into a piece of lemon square then immediately made a sour face. "This is too tart. Don't you guys think so?"

Ruth nodded. "Let's take a bite of Lexy's to see how it compares."

The three other ladies stabbed their forks into the lemon square from Lexy's bakery case.

"This is much sweeter," Ida said.

The others mumbled their agreement and Helen typed more into the iPad.

"I didn't know you wrote for the paper, Helen." Lexy spent a lot of time with the four women and had never heard her mention it before.

"Oh I don't usually, but I have a special spot this month on account of the town bicentennial. They needed some extra reporters," Helen said. "I used to write a food column there when I was younger."

Lexy had almost forgotten about the town bicentennial with its big parade and festival at the end of the week. She'd entered the famous scone bakeoff with her great-grandmother's recipe— she'd have to make sure it came out absolutely perfect if she wanted to compete with this new baker across the street.

"And we're on the historical committee, too," Ida added.

"Oh. That sounds like fun," Lexy said.

"It is. You wouldn't believe all the old dirt we're digging up on this place. Scandals and murders," Ruth whispered. "We're making a display for the festival."

"I tried to get on the baking committee as a judge, but they wouldn't let me because I'm related to Lexy." Nans bristled.

Lexy looked ruefully out the window at *The Brew and Bake*. "That's too bad. I might need a little extra help winning the competition this year."

"Oh, don't be silly," Helen said. "Your baked goods are hands above theirs. Just look at how dry this brownie is."

Helen cut into the brownie, which *did* look rather dry inside. "It's not moist and fudgy like yours."

"That's true," Ruth said following Lexy's glance across the street. "I don't know how the other place is getting more business. I think it has to do with the sewer construction … they've dug up half the sidewalk on this side, making it all but impossible for people to even get to your store."

"Thanks guys." Lexy's heart warmed at their support.

"It's the truth," Ida said, then spit out the piece of éclair she'd bitten into. "Why this éclair is practically rancid. I can't understand why anyone would go to her bakery more than one—"

"Jiminy Crickets, is *that* what I think it is?" Helen's eyes, which had grown as big as moon pies, were riveted on something down the street in the opposite direction of the new bakery. Her mouth hung open in shock revealing the half-chewed brownie inside.

The rest of them quickly swiveled their heads in the direction of Helen's gaze.

Down at the end of the street, all sewer work had stopped. The workers were staring at one man who stood with his bottom-half inside a manhole, his top-half extended out and he was holding something up in his hand.

Nans gasped, the cupcake she'd been holding fell to the table with a light thud.

"Heavens to Betsy ... is he holding a human head?"

Chapter Two

Nans, Ruth, Ida and Helen scrambled out of their chairs, elbowing each other out of the way in their haste to get to the door. Lexy watched them spill out onto the sidewalk as she followed at a more leisurely pace.

The sewer worker was still standing there holding the object, which wasn't a human head per se ... at least not a flesh and blood head. It was a skull—just bone—and from the look of it, had been in the sewer for quite some time.

"Where, exactly, did you find it?" Nans crouched at the edge of the manhole, peering inside.

"It was in the junction there." The man pointed down into the hole. "Must have washed down from further up."

Lexy's gaze followed the man's index finger that pointed in the direction she'd just come from.

"What's up there?" Ida asked.

"The sewer lines run all underneath here. But these bones came from the *old* sewer," the man answered.

"Old sewer?" Ruth echoed.

"The big sections of sewer lines were originally run in the 1930s or 40s. We're replacing most of the lines and blocking off some of the old sections that are in disrepair." The man tapped the skull. "This guy must have been lodged up in there and washed down when we flushed the lines, then got stuck here where the line curves."

Helen leaned over the manhole. "Are there any more bones? I mean the rest of him has gotta be in there, right?"

The man looked down. "Hard to say. The smaller bones probably washed down further, but there could still be some caught up above."

"How big is it down there?" Ida asked. "Can a person get in and walk around?"

"Oh sure," the man replied. "In the main system anyway. It's tall enough to stand in."

"Really?" Nans' sharp green eyes sparkled with interest and she moved toward the ladder the man was standing on. "Let's get down in there and look around."

The man held out his hand. "Sorry. We called the police and they said not to touch a thing. You can't go down there."

Lexy wasn't surprised to see Nans' look of disappointment mirrored in Ruth, Ida and Helen's eyes. The four ladies had an odd hobby—

they were amateur sleuths. They'd helped solve several crimes and even worked closely with the police on a few cases. They'd been instrumental in helping Lexy clear herself when she was accused of poisoning her ex-boyfriend. They even had a name for themselves—*The Ladies Detective Club*.

Lexy knew they wouldn't be able to help themselves from investigating the mysterious skull. And they'd want her to help. The thought caused a trill of excitement to run through her. To tell the truth, she was a bit curious herself and looking for some excitement after her lazy honeymoon with Jack.

A tapping sound pulled Lexy from her thoughts and she turned around to see Victor Nessbaum, the elderly owner of the antique store next to Lexy's bakery, his cane tapping on the sidewalk as he shuffled toward her.

"What's going on?" Victor asked looking from Lexy to Nans to the sewer worker.

"They found a skull in the sewer pipes," Lexy said.

"Skull?" Victor's bushy white eyebrows rose up a fraction of an inch and Lexy motioned toward the sewer worker who held the skull up, then turned it to face them for the first time, revealing the macabre looking thing had two golden teeth right in the front.

Lexy heard Victor gasp and she put a protective arm around him. Victor was in his mid-eighties—not that much older than Nans, but he seemed much frailer. She hoped seeing such a sight wasn't too much of a shock for him.

"Come on, Mr. Nessbaum. Let's get back to our stores." Lexy gently turned the older man around and started back up the sidewalk.

"This darn sewer project is ruining business." Victor gestured to the dug up patches of sidewalk with his cane.

"Tell me about it," Lexy said.

"I'd like to go down to the town hall and give them a piece of my mind. In fact, I'm going to be looking into this very carefully." Victor glanced back over his shoulder at the skull. "The last thing we need is some *investigation* holding up the works and dragging this construction out even longer."

Lexy pressed her lips together. She hadn't thought about that. Would the police shut down the sewer project and leave the sidewalk in shambles?

"Has the new bakery had an impact on your business?" Victor nudged his chin toward *The Brew and Bake.*

"It's hard to tell with the sewer construction going on." Lexy's stomach clenched as she looked back down the street. "Business has dropped off, but most people would find it hard to navigate the sidewalk, so I don't really know if the lull is because people prefer to shop at the new bakery, or if it's simply because they can't *get* to my bakery."

"Well, I hope things pick up for you." Victor frowned at *The Brew and Bake,* his eyes taking on a faraway glassy look. "I can't imagine people preferring her pastries to yours. I don't think she'll be around long. The girl must have no business sense what-so-ever. I mean, who in their right mind would open a bakery directly across the street from one that is already established and successful?"

Chapter Three

Nans and the others came back a few minutes later, their faces flush with excitement. They half-heartedly continued their taste test, but the conversation kept turning to various plans for investigating the mystery of the skull.

Once they'd compared all the baked goods, (Lexy's won hands down,) and Helen had enough for her article, they wrapped up the few leftover pieces of pastry in napkins, shoved them into their over-sized purses and headed on their way.

"Do be sure and find out what Jack knows about the investigation tonight," Nans demanded as she disappeared out the door.

Lexy sat in her empty bakery glaring out the window at *The Brew and Bake*. She could see the perky blonde, who she assumed to be the owner, bustling around inside. Should she go over and introduce herself?

Lexy was debating the pros and cons of introducing herself when police lights at the sewer construction caught her attention.

They sure took their sweet time, she thought as she watched the door of the black sedan open.

Would it be Jack? No. It was Watson Davies, the perky new detective in Jack's squad. Lexy wasn't sure what to make of Davies. She acted like a ditz most of the time, but Lexy had a sneaking suspicion that was an act to catch people off-guard.

Lexy and Davies had gotten off on the wrong foot when Lexy had been caught in the midst of a double murder investigation involving her wedding gown. Everything had worked out in the end, but Lexy wasn't friendly enough with Davies to rush down there and ask a lot of questions. She'd wait for tonight when she was at home with Jack.

At home with Jack.

The thought gave her goose bumps. They'd decided to keep her house, which had originally been Nans', and put Jack's on the market. Even though they'd already spent a lot of time at each other's houses—conveniently located behind one another—the fact they were now going to live together forever made it all seem more thrilling. She couldn't wait to get home every night to be with Jack and, of course, her white Shih-Tzu mix, Sprinkles.

Tearing herself away from the window, she walked over to the bakery case. A sugary treat would sure help alleviate the boredom. She'd given Cassie the day off and being at the bakery alone with few customers to wait on left her with only two things to do to fill her time—bake and eat.

Glancing at her reflection in the chrome display-case door, she pushed at a lock of brown hair that had escaped the ponytail that swung just below her shoulders. Her face was still tanned from lazy days in the sun and it made her green eyes look even lighter than usual. She slid the door open and picked out a chocolate whoopee pie. Leaning on the top of the case she bit into the chocolaty confection, savoring the contrasting flavors of dark chocolate and the sweet creamy middle.

As she chewed, she contemplated what to do next. The police had the street almost blocked off now and she doubted any customers would be coming by. Maybe today was a good day to close early, go home and make a nice home-cooked meal for Jack. She could even bring his favorite pie—coconut cream.

Shoving the rest of the whoopee pie into her mouth, she opened the refrigerated display case that held the pies, pulled out a coconut cream, set it in a pie box on top of the case and then rearranged the pie display to fill in the empty space.

Grabbing a clean cloth, she swiped at the few crumbs left on the cafe tables on her way to the front door where she hesitated for a few seconds, her hand hovering over the lock.

Lexy never closed the shop early, but felt certain keeping it open today was a waste of time. Even though she hated to miss out on even one customer, the time would be better spent at home unwinding and unpacking after her trip. Her mind made up, she grabbed the sign on the door and quickly turned it over to the "Closed" side.

Turning away from the door, her eyes drifted across the street and her heart stuttered when she found herself looking right into the beady blue eyes of the blonde at *The Brew and Bake*. She stood frozen for a split second.

Should she wave?

No, the other woman did not look friendly at all.

Lexy ripped her gaze away and then spun around, turning off the lights and grabbing the pie on her way out the back door. She'd meet the owner of *The Brew and Bake* some other time—Lexy was sure of it.

***

"So, tell me about the skull they found in the sewer pipes today." Lexy slid the piece of pie across the kitchen table to Jack and leaned back in her chair as he stabbed his fork into it.

Jack closed his eyes, swirling the pie around in his mouth and making *nummy* noises.

"There's not much to tell." He took another forkful of pie and held it up to his mouth. "The skull belongs to a male. It's been down there for a long time."

"How long?"

"We're not exactly sure but the medical examiner said probably decades." Jack broke off a piece of piecrust and held it out for Sprinkles, who twirled around in excitement before inhaling it.

"Wow. That's a long time." Lexy gathered the dinner dishes from the table to load into the dishwasher.

"We have some people going down tomorrow to see if they can come up with any more bones or figure out what happened, but it's a long-shot we'll be able to find out too much and the case isn't a priority."

Lexy spun around to face him. "What do you mean? You're not going to hold up the sewer project are you?"

Jack raised a brow at her. "Well, I don't know. Technically, we shouldn't disturb anything but, like I said, most of the evidence is probably gone by now. The site is so old. I know there is a lot of pressure to get that project done and the street patched back up before the bicentennial though, so I doubt our investigation would hold up the project too much."

"So, if you don't find anything tomorrow, you just drop it?" Lexy asked incredulously. Surely, they would investigate until they found out how the skull got there, wouldn't they?

"Oh, no." Jack brought his empty pie plate over to the dishwasher. "There are other entrances to the old sewer system and we can still have the sewer commission open up the manholes later on so we can get in that way."

"Oh, good. I'm losing business with that street all dug up like that. Not to mention the new bakery."

"Surely, you aren't worried about the competition." Jack stepped closer, his arm snaking around her back to untie her apron.

No, not really. Was she?

"No, but …"

Jack pulled her close. She leaned into him inhaling his clean, spicy scent.

"You know you make the best pastries around. I'm sure that other bakery's stuff isn't nearly as good." He tugged on her ponytail, freeing her hair which cascaded down around her shoulders.

"That's what Nans and the gang said." Lexy pressed her lips together. "But I better make sure these scones I have entered in the bake-off are absolutely perfect. I may need to do some test runs. They *have* to be good enough to beat her entry."

"Your great-grandma's recipe?" Jack tugged on her hand, pulling her toward the door leading to the living room.

"Yeah. It always wins top prize." Lexy followed him absently, her mind on the torn up sidewalks, the competing bakery across the street and making sure she baked *the* winning scones.

"I'm sure you'll win with those. They're delicious." Jack continued pulling her toward the stairs. "And so are you …"

"Huh?" She looked up at him then flushed when she recognized the primal look in his eye. "Oh."

Jack smiled and Lexy realized they were at the bottom of the stairs … which wasn't such a bad thing.

"Well, even if the police don't have time to investigate the mysterious skull, I know four ladies who do," Lexy said.

Jack turned looking at her pointedly. "Four … or five?"

Lexy grimaced. In the past, Jack hadn't always approved of her helping Nans and *The Ladies Detective Club* with their investigations. Lately, though, he'd loosened up a bit. She hoped he wouldn't get mad at her if she helped out on this one. "Well, it does seem kind of intriguing … I mean a decades-old skeleton in a sewer system—who wouldn't want to investigate that?"

Jack laughed. "You and Nans might as well go ahead. Like I said, it's not a priority for us. We have a backlog of *recent* murders to investigate."

Lexy stopped short. "Murders? You mean the man who belonged to the skull was murdered?"

"We don't know for sure, but judging by the hole in the middle of his head I'd have to say murder is a definite possibility."

Chapter Four

"I think she's up to something." Cassie glanced out the window toward *The Brew and Bake,* the magenta tips of her spiky short blonde hair seemed to glow in the sun streaming through the window.

"Really? Why do you say that?" Lexy looked up from the old cookbook she held in her hands. The yellowed pages were dotted with stains and the binding bulged with various recipes handwritten on paper and index cards or ripped from magazines. One of her most prized possessions, the collection had been in her family since her great-grandmother, with each new generation adding to it.

"I can't say for sure, but don't you think it's weird someone would open a bakery right across from another bakery?"

"I suppose so, but maybe she's just not very smart."

Cassie pressed her lips together. "There's something else."

"What?"

"I'm pretty sure I saw her sneaking around out back near our dumpster the other day."

"The dumpster? What would she want out there?"

Cassie shrugged. "Who knows? Maybe to find out something about the ingredients we use or something?"

Or find notes for some of my recipes, Lexy thought, looking back down at the cookbook.

"All the more reason for me to make sure I win the baking contest in the bicentennial," Lexy said. "Then the whole town will know our bakery is the best."

"When is Helen's article coming out in the paper?" Cassie asked.

"Good question. That should help business along. I'll have to call Nans and find out."

"No need to call, you can just ask her yourself." Cassie jerked her chin toward the door that had just swung open to reveal Nans, Ruth, Ida and Helen.

"Hi 'ya, girls!" Nans yelled out a greeting on her way to the pastry case.

Lexy and Cassie greeted the four older women, then grabbed an assortment of pastries from the bakery cases and brought them to the tables.

"So, when is your article coming out, Helen?" Lexy asked once everyone was seated with a cup of steaming coffee or tea and the array of pastries in front of them.

Helen broke off a piece of blueberry scone. "It's supposed to be Wednesday. I don't think the owner of the other bakery is going to like it much."

"Oh?" Cassie raised a pierced brow at Helen.

"Their goods are not as tasty as Lexy's. I did an in-depth comparison and simply told the truth in my article. I have several factors I judged them on and Lexy's came out as far superior." Helen shrugged then added hastily. "And it's not just because she's Nans' granddaughter, either."

Lexy slid her eyes over to *The Brew and Bake*. She could see a couple of customers milling around inside but it was nothing like the day before, even though her sign still announced a fifty-percent off sale. She watched the door open. A familiar figure shuffled out, cane in one hand and grocery bag in the other.

Victor Nessbaum. *The traitor!*

Lexy watched him amble across the street, dangling his cane from the wrist of the hand that held the bag while he put something in his pocket with the other hand. Lexy wondered why he had gone to the other bakery when the day before she had gotten the feeling he didn't approve. Maybe the lure of getting fifty-percent off was too great.

"So, Lexy, were you able to get any information out of Jack about the skull?" Nans' eager voice pulled her attention from the window.

"Not too much. He said the police were going into the sewer lines today to look for the rest of the bones and any evidence," Lexy said. "Oh, and he did say the skull was from a man and they suspect he was murdered."

Ida gasped. "I *knew* it!"

Ruth rubbed her hands together. "This is very exciting ... maybe we can integrate his murder into the display we are making for the bicentennial."

"We'll need to research it first of course," Nans said.

"Naturally," Helen added.

"Where do we start?" Ida asked.

"If only we could get into the sewer." Ruth craned her neck toward the end of the street where they had found the skull.

"Maybe once the police are done, we can talk to the sewer workers," Nans said.

"John said they were going to be done today and then the sewer workers could finish up in a couple of days," Cassie added. She'd heard about the skull from her husband John, also a homicide detective.

"Jack said there's other ways to get into the sewers, too," Lexy said, then immediately regretted it. She wasn't sure she liked the idea of her grandmother crawling around in the sewer.

Nans' face lit up. "Really? Did he say where?"

"Nooo." Lexy drew the word out.

"Well, that's no help," Ida said. "Maybe we can go to the town hall and look up the blueprints. That's what they always do on TV."

"We need to go down there anyway to do some more research for the historical society display," Ruth added.

"Which reminds me ..." Nans rummaged inside her purse, pulled out a piece of paper and handed it to Lexy. "... we found this newspaper article showing your great-grandma winning the Brook Ridge Falls Octoberfest with her famous scones, so all those times she bragged about the recipe being a sure-fire contest winner she wasn't just shining us on!"

Lexy's heart warmed as she looked at the paper. She had vague, but fond memories of her great-grandmother who had died when she was eight. The picture showed a younger version of great-grandma, proudly holding a blue ribbon.

"Boy I wish she were here to help me make the scones for the contest," Lexy said.

"Oh, don't worry dear." Nans patted her hand. "You're a wonderful baker. You'll make the prize-winning scones and you'll certainly beat out the *other* bakery."

"Of course, and I have great-grandma's recipe right here." Lexy fingered a dog-eared yellow piece of paper that stuck out from the edge of the book. "Actually, I think I'll go back to the kitchen right now and make a practice batch."

She stood, clutching the book to her chest. "Cassie, can you watch the front?"

"Of course."

"Thanks." Lexy started toward the back. She *should* feel good. After all, she had the recipe that had proven to win dozens of contests for both her great-grandmother and herself. Plus, she knew the baked items at the other place didn't even taste that good.

So, why did she feel less than confident?

Maybe it was because of what Cassie had said about seeing the other owner out at the dumpster. That seemed to indicate she wasn't just someone who didn't have the business smarts to not open a bakery across the street from an established one, but that she was *actively* trying to compete with Lexy.

But *why* would she do that?

Lexy couldn't come up with a good reason. On her way to the kitchen, Lexy peered out at the dumpster.

Was there information to be gained by looking through another bakery's dumpster?

Lexy had no idea, but she also had no intention of letting the other baker get the upper hand.

Two could play at the dumpster diving game.

***

The scent of butter and sugar from an afternoon of baking scones hung in the air around Lexy and Cassie as they crouched down in the darkness of the front room of *The Cup and Cake*.

"Is she ever going to leave?" Cassie hissed peeking up over the edge of the window to look across the street at *The Brew and Bake*.

Lexy shifted her position in an attempt to stop her legs from cramping. It was almost eight o'clock and they'd closed down *The Cup and Cake* over an hour ago.

Lexy pulled the black knit hat down across her forehead, then looked up over the edge of the window. Across the street, the blonde bustled around her cafe tables, wiping them down and rearranging the napkin and sugar holders. Lexy's heart skipped and she quickly ducked back down when the other woman glanced out toward her.

"I don't think she can see us. It's pitch black in here," Cassie said as if reading Lexy's mind. "Thank God, she's turning the sign on the door."

Lexy poked her head back up in time to see the blonde turn the sign to "Closed" and grab her coat from a coat rack beside the door before turning off the light and exiting the shop.

"Let's go." Lexy scurried to the back door. The two of them crept outside, then ran across the street like shadows in their identical head-to-toe all-black outfits.

It had turned cold after sunset. Puddles topped with thin ice crunched under Lexy's black boots as she slipped along the side of *The Brew and Bake* and made a beeline for the dumpster.

"What are we looking for?" Cassie whispered.

"I don't know, but if she looked in our dumpster, it's only fair we look in hers. There must be something one can find out by looking in your competitor's dumpster, but I guess we won't know until we find it."

Lexy eyed the dumpster. It was one of the smaller ones and she could see over the edge without having to get up on anything; except it was hard to see anything in there in the dark.

"Did you bring a flashlight?" Lexy asked.

Cassie answered by snapping on a small light and aiming a thin beam into the dumpster.

"What is all this ... It looks like just a bunch of cardboard boxes." Lexy heaved herself up on the side, balancing like a seesaw on her hipbones. She reached into the dumpster lifting one of the boxes to flip it over. Her breath caught in her throat when she saw the lettering.

"These are from the grocery store!" She picked one up and tossed it out to Cassie.

"That scammer! Do you think she's buying baked goods at the grocery store and passing them off as hers?" Cassie asked.

Lexy rummaged through the pile to see if she could find anything else, but the only things in there were more boxes along with something gooey and sticky which made her thankful she was wearing gloves. She slid off the side of the dumpster before answering her friend's question.

"Well, it sure seems like she has a lot of grocery store bakery boxes, but why would she open a bakery and then try to pass off grocery store goods?"

Cassie frowned down at the box in her hand. "I have no idea—"

"Shhhh." Lexy heard a click coming from the direction of the back door and cut Cassie off.

She pulled Cassie behind the dumpster in a crouch. Lexy craned her neck to peer around the end of the dumpster just as a slice of light spilled out from the opening door. She jerked her head back and leaned against the cold metal.

"...figure out a way to get access across the street," a man's voice said.

More boxes clanged into the dumpster causing the girls to cringe. Lexy's heart hammered in her chest, her breath came out in short puffs of condensation. Beside her, Cassie rubbed her arms, her nose was red from the cold.

"That's going to be hard. But I have an idea. Maybe we can..." The woman's voice was cut off by the door shutting behind them as they went inside.

Lexy exchanged a wide-eyed look with Cassie. Across the street? Did they mean her bakery?

"Let's get out of here before they come back out." Cassie ventured a look over the top of the dumpster.

Lexy nodded and the two girls ran for the side of the building, then across the street to the safety of *The Cup and Cake*.

"What was that about?" Lexy unlocked the back door to her bakery.

"Sounded like they want to get into your bakery."

"Yeah, it sure did." Lexy looked around the gleaming stainless steel kitchen. "But, what could they possibly want in here? And who was that guy?"

Cassie shrugged. "Maybe he is her business partner. My guess is they want your scones recipe. If they can win the contest it would lend a lot of credibility to their bakery ... even if it is full of repurposed grocery store items."

Lexy pressed her lips together. Winning the contest *would* give the bakery credibility, but surely, they couldn't want to run a bakery *that* bad. She knew from experience the bakery business was no road to easy riches—it required a lot of hard work for very little money. And if you don't like baking in the first place, which it seems the people over at *The Brew and Bake* didn't, then what was the point?

She grabbed her purse and wool navy blue pea coat from the coat rack where she kept the vintage aprons she liked to wear. She hadn't wanted to explain her dumpster diving plans to Jack, so she'd told him she and Cassie were going out for some "girl time" after work. He would be expecting her home soon.

"I guess we'd better be going." Lexy shoved her arms through the sleeves of her coat then the two of them went back out the door to where their cars were parked behind the bakery.

Lexy glanced across the narrow parking lot toward *The Brew and Bake*. "I have a funny feeling something strange is going on over there— it seems like someone is going to an awful lot of trouble just to win a baking contest for a bakery that doesn't even bake its own pastries."

Chapter Five

The next morning, Lexy noticed the sewer workers were back in full force. They'd closed down the street, causing her to take a detour to get to the bakery from the other end of the road.

Walking from her car to the back door of the bakery, she resigned herself to another day of low sales. At least the other bakery would suffer the same predicament, since the whole street was blocked off this time.

She figured the sewer workers were putting in an extra effort to make up for the lost day yesterday, which reminded her that Nans would be coming to grill her about any information Jack had given up regarding the skull. She'd better hurry if she wanted to get scones baked and sugar cookie dough out of the freezer to thaw before she got sidetracked with Nans.

Focused on her thoughts, Lexy didn't notice the door hanging slightly open until she tried to insert her key and the door swung inward without her even having to unlock it.

Her blood froze as her eyes registered the splintered wood around the lock—someone had broken in!

She stood in the doorway for a few seconds and then took two tentative steps inside.

"Hello?"

No one answered, so she made her way toward the kitchen, her heart sinking when she saw the mess. Cookbooks lay spread open and her recipe box had been torn apart. Recipes lay in messy piles on the counters and spilling onto the floor.

Reaching in her coat pocket for her cell phone, she ran to the front of the store expecting to see smashed display cases and food all over the place, but the front room looked just as she'd left it the night before. Either whoever broke in had run out of time and never made it to the front room, or they'd found whatever they were looking for in the kitchen and didn't need to look further.

Her shaky fingers managed to find Jack on her contacts list and she pressed the button to call him.

"Perillo," he answered in the voice he reserved for police business.

"Jack, it's me," Lexy said in a rushed, breathless voice. "The bakery's been broken into!"

"What?" Lexy could hear alarm in Jack's voice. "Are you okay?"

"Yes, I came in this morning and the door had been broken. The kitchen's messed up, but the front room is okay. I guess whoever did it is long gone." Lexy glanced across the street at *The Brew and Bake.*

"Okay, you stay put and I'll be right over with a crime unit," Jack said, then added, "And don't touch anything."

Lexy heard a sound behind her and whirled around just in time to see Cassie stop short in front of the opening to the kitchen.

"What the heck?" Cassie's mouth fell open. She turned wide eyes in Lexy's direction.

"Looks like we've been broken into," Lexy said. "The lock on the back door was jimmied."

"What? Why?" Cassie sputtered. "Did they take anything?"

"I don't know ... Jack said not to touch anything, but I don't think it can hurt if we look around a little."

Lexy followed Cassie back into the kitchen. "What a mess."

"I don't see anything missing. I mean the blenders are all here, the equipment is in place." Cassie gestured around the room. "The only thing out of place is all this paper."

"The recipes."

Cassie frowned down at the pile on the floor. "Wait. You don't think …?

"I sure do."

Best friends since high school, the girls had an uncanny way of being able to read each other's thoughts. She knew Cassie referred to the conversation they'd heard behind the dumpster.

"We heard them say they needed to get in here just last night," Lexy said. "And then this morning we come in to *this*. I don't think that's a coincidence."

"Not to mention, it looks like they were only interested in your recipes," Cassie pointed out.

Lexy's heart crunched when she thought of her grandmother's handwritten scone recipe. Sure, she had a copy of it on her computer, but she still didn't want her competitor getting a hold of the recipe. Besides the original recipe written in her grandmother's hand had sentimental value.

She bent down to pick the recipes off the floor and then remembered Jack's warning. "Crap, Jack said not to touch things, so I guess I better leave these here. But it won't hurt to at least *look* at them to see if the scone recipe is gone."

"Right," Cassie agreed.

The girls sifted carefully through the piles with Lexy taking the floor and Cassie the counters.

"Hey, I think I found it!" Lexy pointed at a yellowed piece of paper turning her head sideways to read it. "Yes! That's it."

"So, they didn't take it?"

"I guess not." Lexy frowned at the paper. Maybe they'd written out a copy? But it didn't make sense they'd take the time to do that.

Something shiny under the cabinet caught her eye.

"Hey. What's this?" She reached under the cabinet to retrieve the item—a gold and pearl ring which she held up to show Cassie. "Did you lose this?"

"No."

"Lose what?" A voice squeaked from the doorway. Lexy turned to see Detective Watson Davies standing there with Jack right behind her.

"Detective Davies. Nice to see you again," Lexy said.

"Same here." Davies jaw worked up and down on a piece of gum. Lexy couldn't help but notice Davies' fashionable buckle-studded black leather boots. The woman did have excellent taste in footwear.

"So, are you tampering with evidence again?" Davies nodded toward the ring.

"Oh, sorry." Lexy grimaced. "I found it on the floor and thought it was Cassie's."

"But it's not." Davies looked at Cassie who shook her head.

"And you don't know who else it could belong to?"

Lexy shook *her* head.

"Do a lot of people have access to the kitchen?"

"No."

"Then it might belong to whoever broke in," Davies pointed out.

"Right." Lexy gingerly placed the ring in Davies' glove-clad palm while trying to keep from getting fingerprints all over it.

"I guess we should start making a list of what was taken," Jack said.

"Well, that's the thing." Lexy looked around the room one more time. "Nothing *was* taken."

"What?" Davies scrunched up her face. "Who breaks in to a place and doesn't take anything? Did you check the cash register? What do you have of value here?"

"We cash out every night. The appliances are valuable, but they're all accounted for. The only thing that's out of place is the recipes." Lexy gestured toward the counter and floor.

"So, you're trying to tell us someone broke in for recipes?" Davies asked. "Who would do that?"

"I'm pretty sure I know who," Lexy said. "In fact, I bet if we take that ring across the street we'll find out who it belongs to and you'll have your thief."

***

"I don't think you should be coming over here with me," Davies said as she stomped across the street, the plastic bag holding the ring dangling from her hand.

"What if I just happened to want to go over to get a muffin or brownie?" Lexy knew Davies was right, but she just *had* to see the other baker's reaction when caught red-handed. Luckily, Jack had already left after assuring himself Lexy was okay—he never would have allowed her to accompany the detective to question the other baker.

Davies sighed and rolled her eyes before wrenching the shop door open, causing a cacophony of bells to jingle.

The blonde stood behind the counter, handing a bakery box to a customer. She jerked her head in Davies' direction as if sensing danger, her eyes widening at the sight of the badge-wielding Detective with Lexy at her side.

"Can I help you?" The blonde glanced nervously at the customer who hurried to the door. Lexy noticed the sugary-vanilla scent of baked goods wafting in the air and wondered how that could be possible if the baker bought all her goods from the grocery store. Maybe she used vanilla scented candles or potpourri? Lexy pictured pots of baking scented potpourri simmering on the stove out back.

"I'm Detective Watson Davies..." Davies flashed the badge in her face. "...and this is Lexy Baker."

"Perillo," Lexy corrected.

"Right. Baker-Perillo." Davies shot an annoyed glance at Lexy.

"Caraleigh Brewster." The blonde's brow creased slightly as she stepped out from behind the bakery case to shake hands with both of them "What is this about?"

"Are you aware that Ms. Baker ... err ... Mrs. Perillo's bakery was broken into last night?" Davies asked.

"What?" Caraleigh seemed genuinely distraught. "I had no idea."

"Really?" Davies cocked an eyebrow at Caraleigh and held up the bag with the ring. "Is this your ring?"

Caraleigh's hand flew to her chest. "Yes ... I noticed it was missing just yesterday. Where did you find it?"

"It was found in Lexy's bakery," Davies said.

Caraleigh's icy blue glare pierced Lexy. "You stole my ring?"

"What?" Lexy narrowed her eyes at the blonde. How dare she accuse Lexy when *she* was the thief! Lexy drew herself up to her full five-foot-four-inch height and took a step closer to Caraleigh. "No. You dropped it when you broke in to *my* bakery to steal *my* recipes."

"Recipes?" Caraleigh stepped closer to Lexy. The taller woman leaned down so their faces were inches apart. "I didn't steal any recipes. What are you talking about?"

"Hold it." Davies pushed them apart, shooting a warning glance first at Lexy and then Caraleigh.

Caraleigh planted her fists on her hips. "Just what, exactly, is going on here, Detective?"

"Well, Ms. Brewster, it seems likely you lost this ring during the robbery."

"The robbery where they stole recipes? Why would I steal recipes ...? I obviously have plenty of my own." Caraleigh spread her arms to indicate the bakery cases full of pastries.

Lexy squinted into the cases. *Had she baked the items or bought them at the grocery store?* She leaned closer to see if she could recognize any of the desserts as being from the grocery. They looked similar, but it seemed like Caraleigh had fancied them up with additional frosting and adornments.

"Err ... well, actually we don't think they stole anything," Davies admitted peevishly. "But someone definitely broke in and your ring was found there. Can you explain that?"

"Maybe Ms. Baker here did it herself to frame me," Caraleigh huffed.

"That's ridiculous!" Lexy's face flushed with anger. "Why would I do that? And how would I get your ring?"

"Why would you frame me?" Caraleigh asked. "Maybe because you feel threatened I'm taking all your business away. As to how you would get my ring, I think I have a pretty good idea."

"Oh, I'd love to hear that." Lexy crossed her arms across her chest.

"Me too," Davies said.

"I noticed my ring was missing yesterday, right after I had a visit from your neighbor," Caraleigh said.

"My neighbor?"

"The old guy who owns the antique store." Caraleigh pointed across the street. "I bet the two of you are in cahoots. Somehow, he stole my ring and the two of you set it up. Although I can't say what his motivation would be ... unless maybe you were paying him."

Lexy glanced at Davies, her heart sinking when she realized the detective was actually considering Caraleigh's explanation.

"It's plausible, but seems a little far-fetched don't you think?" Davies asked.

"No, I don't," Caraleigh answered. "Not only *that,* but I can prove I didn't break in. I have an airtight alibi."

"Oh?" Davies' brows raised a fraction of an inch.

"Yes. I was at the television station WOKQ talking to Pierce Daniels about a segment they are doing on my bakery. About a dozen witnesses can verify I was there until midnight. My brother can verify I came straight home after the interview."

Davies whipped out her cell phone and tapped a note into it. "I'll have to verify those. Where can I find your brother?"

"We're new in town, so we're sharing an apartment at the Westlake Village. Number twenty-ten. His name his Harvey Brewster." Caraleigh said indignantly.

"Okay, I'll check up on this and get back to you … both of you." Davies turned to leave.

Lexy glared at Caraleigh for a few seconds before following Davies to the door.

"Oh, and detective?" Caraleigh yelled after them causing Davies to turn around. "Next time, you should think about doing a more thorough job before accusing innocent people. I don't appreciate it and if it happens again … I'll have your badge."

Lexy bit her lip at Davies' outraged look, but the detective didn't get a chance to say anything before Caraleigh opened her mouth and spoke again, this time to Lexy.

"And you, Ms. Baker, better mind your own business … while you still have a business left to mind."

Chapter Six

Lexy struggled to keep a lid on her anger as she stomped back across the street to her own bakery. The back door hung open and she bent down to inspect the area around the lock, now covered with black fingerprint dust. She'd have to call someone to have it replaced right away.

"How did it go? Did she confess?" Cassie stood in the doorway eyeing Lexy and Davies excitedly.

"No, she denied it. Claims she has an airtight alibi," Lexy said rolling her eyes.

"I'll be checking that out today," Davies said. "In the meantime, you guys are free to clean all this up and get back to business as usual. We dusted the lock for fingerprints, but I doubt we'll get anything from it."

"That's all you're going to do?" Lexy stared at Davies.

"Well, since there was nothing stolen, there's not much *for* us to do." Davies looked at the broken door, then out into the back parking lot. "We'll try to figure out who broke in, but unfortunately, in the grand scheme of things, this is going to be a very low priority."

"But what about the ring?" Lexy asked.

"We'll keep that as evidence while I check out Caraleigh's alibi." Davies looked at her watch. "I gotta run, but I'll try to swing by tomorrow with an update."

"At least she's not quite as abrasive as she was the last time you had to deal with her," Cassie said as they watched Davies retreat to her car.

"Yeah, but it doesn't seem like she's going to be very helpful," Lexy added.

"She'll come through once Caraleigh's alibi doesn't pan out," Cassie said.

"Will it *not* pan out though? Caraleigh seemed pretty confident."

"But we know she did it—"

The bells jingling on the front door interrupted Cassie, and Lexy's spirits picked up. "Sounds like we have a customer!"

The girls rushed to the front room. Lexy felt a minor tinge of disappointment to see Nans, Ruth, Ida, and Helen come through the door instead of the throng of paying customers she was hoping for.

"Did I just see the police leaving here?" Nans asked.

"Yes." Lexy told her about the break-in and their suspicions it was the bakery owner across the street.

"What makes you think it was her?" Nans asked.

Cassie and Lexy exchanged a sheepish glance. "We kind of heard her say that she needed to get in here."

"Kind of?" Nans' brows creased as she eyed Lexy.

"We took a little trip over there last night to peek in her dumpster and heard Caraleigh and some man talking."

"Oh, that sounds exciting." Nans' eyes sparkled. "I wish you'd called me to go with you."

"So, did you tell Davies you overheard her?" Ida asked.

"Well, that's the thing." Lexy sighed. "We really can't tell her because then we'd have to reveal we were sneaking around back there and it could make us look suspicious. As it was, Caraleigh accused *me* of planting the ring to incriminate *her*!"

"Oh, the nerve. Now why did she think you would do that?" Helen asked.

"I wouldn't." Lexy answered. "But I did find out something else interesting."

"What?" The four ladies chorused.

"Her dumpster was loaded with boxes from the grocery store bakery. I think she's just loading her cases up with purchased goods."

Helen gasped. "That scammer! I knew her stuff didn't have that home-baked taste of a small bakery!"

"But *why* would she do that? And *why* break in here?" Ruth asked.

"Well, they went through the cookbooks and recipe files, so I assume they were after recipes." Lexy shrugged. "Great-grandma's scone recipe is still there, thankfully."

"Wait a minute; if she's buying the pastries at the grocery and putting them in her case, then why would she need recipes?" Ida asked.

"That's a good question," Helen said to Ida as she picked out an herbal tea from the self-serve station. "There's something funny going on in Denmark."

"Denmark?" Ruth looked at Helen. "What's that got to do with anything?"

"Just an expression, dear."

"So, how about we try out some of those scones?" Nans said to distract Ruth and Helen from the argument they were teetering on the brink of.

"Oh, right. I baked some yesterday and I'm trying a variation this afternoon." Lexy stood and started toward the kitchen. "It would be great if you guys could try both and let me know which you prefer."

In the kitchen, Cassie had already cleaned up the recipes and was busy mixing up the dough for peanut butter cookies. Lexy inhaled the comforting, sweet, nutty aroma that hung in the air as she piled some scones on a platter for Nans and the other ladies.

"I figure I'd do some baking and keep the cases stocked with fresh cookies ... for when the customers come back," Cassie said.

"Yeah, I'm sure sales will be back to normal as soon as the sewer project is done and people can actually get to the store," Lexy said. "I'll watch the front room and you can bake, then this afternoon we'll switch."

"Sounds good." Cassie returned to her mixing. "Oh, and I called someone to fix the lock."

"Perfect. Thanks." Lexy shot Cassie a grateful smile, then took the platter out front and placed it on the table in front of the ladies. She grabbed a coffee while the women each picked a scone and loaded it on their plate.

"I made these scones to put in the bakery case, but I don't think too many customers will be coming in to buy them," Lexy said ruefully.

"Oh now, dear, I'm sure that's not true," Nans said. "Once the big sale is over at the other bakery and the people get a taste of how stale her baked goods are, they'll be back here."

"Especially after they read my article," Helen said.

Lexy pulled a chair up to the table and sat. Wrapping her palm around the warm mug of coffee, she reveled in the refreshingly bitter aroma steaming up from the mug and glanced across the street at the line of customers in the *other* bakery.

"I sure hope so." Lexy turned her back to the window and leaned her elbows on the table. "Let's talk about something else."

"We're making great headway on our display for the bicentennial," Nans said scooping a chocolate chip out of her scone with her fork. "In fact, we've dug up the most fascinating piece of town history."

"That's right. It's got everything one could want—interesting characters, illegal doings, money, greed, robbery and even a romance." Ida ticked the items off on her fingers.

"Really?" Lexy's brows shot up. "Do tell."

Ida leaned in, lowering her voice even though no one was in the shop to overhear her. "Well, you see, back in 1948 the Second Regional Bank here in town was robbed. By Brook Ridge Falls' very own band of gangsters."

"Brook Ridge Falls had gangsters?"

"Yep," Nans answered. "And they had cool names too ... like 'Midas Mulcahey' and 'The Bomb'."

"Anyway," Ida continued, "they made off with almost a million dollars in bills and gold bars."

"And there was a mysterious woman involved, too." Ruth winked.

"Almost like Bonnie and Clyde, except these guys got away with it," Helen added.

"They were never heard from again." Nans' green eyes danced mischievously over her cup of tea.

"Probably off spending the money," Ida said. "Don't you think that will make a great display for the historical commission table?"

Lexy nodded. "Sounds like fun."

"Of course, we still have more research to do, but we don't want to spend all our time on *that* when we have the murder of the skull to solve," Nans said.

Lexy looked out the window where the sewer workers were busy doing their job. "How is that going?"

"Ruth looked at the police records going way back, but didn't find any missing persons who haven't been located," Nans said. "So we don't have much to go on."

"Maybe the police have found out more about it since they went down into the sewers." Ruth looked at Lexy hopefully. "You could ask Jack."

"Sure, I can ask him tonight," Lexy said. "But, I think he said it's not a big priority, so I don't know if I'll be able to get any useful information."

"All the more reason for us to look into it ourselves," Nans said. "But we'd better hurry. If they're closing off all the entrances to the old sewer pipes with this new project, we may not have much time left until our access is cut off.

Chapter Seven

The rest of the day was uneventful and not very profitable even though they did manage to get a handful of customers. Lexy immersed herself in perfecting the scone recipe and, by the time the day ended, she was more than ready to get out of the kitchen.

She'd made plans with Jack to meet at his house. There was still a lot of work to do before they could put it up for sale, so she grabbed some frosted brownies from the case and aimed her car toward *The Burger Barn* to pick up take-out before heading home.

Parking at her own house, she ran inside, her heart flooding with warmth at Sprinkles' enthusiastic greeting, which she wasn't exactly sure was for her or the white take-out bag full of burgers and fries.

"Hi, Sprinkles." Lexy put the box of brownies and take-out bag on the counter, and then bent down and ruffled the dog behind her ears while trying to dodge the pink tongue that insisted on licking Lexy's face. "We're going to go over to Jack's and eat, okay?"

Sprinkles spun in circles, and then ran to the back door. Lexy picked the white bag off the counter, opened the door and stepped out onto her frosty patio, then made her way across her back yard, through the fence and across Jack's back yard to his kitchen door.

Lexy gave a quick tap on the window and opened the door. The kitchen was empty, but the basement door stood ajar and Lexy could see the lights were on downstairs.

"Hello?" Lexy yelled down.

"Down here!" Jack's voice answered from below. Sprinkles let out a yelp then bounded down the stairs. Lexy put the takeout bag on the counter and followed.

Jack's house was small and, even though the basement ran the whole length of the house, it seemed smaller because of all the boxes, old furniture and piles of junk that were crammed into every inch of space. The low ceiling made it seem even smaller. A few bare bulbs had been placed in white ceramic sockets that hung from the ceiling to provide light that added to the cave-like feel. Lexy's lungs itched as she breathed in mildew, dust and cobwebs.

Jack stood in the middle of a pile of boxes, his shirt smudged with dirt. Sprinkles was busy sniffing around his feet.

"How on earth did you amass this much stuff?" Lexy gestured toward the towering piles. "You've only been living here for seven years."

Jack puffed out his cheeks. "Actually, most of it is from the previous owners. It was all here when I moved in."

Lexy picked her way toward him. "I remember Nans said they lived here since it was built in 1940."

"Yeah, they were a sweet old couple," Jack said. "They were going to senior living and didn't know what to do with all this stuff, so I told them just to leave it. Figured maybe I'd have a use for some of it someday."

Lexy peeked inside a box loaded with vintage turquoise kitchenware. "Jeez it's like a time capsule from the 1950s in here."

"Yeah, they saved everything." Jack stepped sideways and motioned to several piles of newspapers and magazines.

"Sheesh." Lexy bent over to examine one of the piles. "Hey, these are local papers from the 1940s ... I wonder if they have the papers from 1948."

"Feel free to take a look." Jack gestured to the pile before turning his attention back to the old tools he had been unpacking from a box.

Lexy squatted and flipped through the yellowed newspapers. Some of the pages were brittle and the edges flaked off in her fingers. The piles were stacked in chronological order, so it didn't take long for her to find the ones from 1948. She pulled them out of the stack.

"Can I take these for Nans?"

Jack looked up at her, his right brow rose a fraction of an inch. "For Nans? What is she up to now?"

"The ladies are doing some historical society project for the bicentennial and it has something to do with some big robbery that happened in 1948."

Jack shrugged. "Take whatever you want. It's all gotta go somewhere."

Lexy set the papers aside and wiped her dirty hands on her jeans. Looking around the basement at all the junk they had to go through made her feel overwhelmed. She needed food.

"Let's take a break and eat," she suggested. "I brought take-out from *The Burger Barn* and it's getting cold on your counter."

"Sounds good." Jack smiled at her. "But first ... I think you look a little too clean."

She squealed as he reached over to pull her close, his hands leaving dirty handprints on the sleeves of her shirt. He smudged his finger on her nose, then his warm lips descended on hers almost making her forget they were in the dirty, dingy, spider-filled basement.

Until something rubbed against her leg.

Lexy screeched and jumped back. Looking down expecting to find a giant spider, she breathed a sigh of relief to see it was only Sprinkles. Jack laughed then bent down to pet the dog. "Come on you two, let's go eat."

The three of them went up the stairs. Lexy pulled plates, glasses and silverware out of the cabinets and drawers, then plopped a burger on each plate and set them on the table. Taking the fries out of the bag, she divvied them up between the plates and gave one teensy piece to an overjoyed Sprinkles.

Jack poured milk into the glasses and they settled down at the old Formica kitchen table.

"Did you find out anything more about the break-in at the bakery?" Jack asked as he lifted the burger to his mouth.

"You won't believe this." Lexy poured ketchup on her burger. "Davies brought the ring over to Caraleigh and she admitted it was hers, but said it had been stolen!"

"Caraleigh is the lady that owns the other bakery?" Jack asked.

"Yes. She said she had an alibi for last night and actually had the nerve to accuse me of stealing the ring from her, then faking the break-in and planting the ring!"

"Seriously? What did she think your motivation for doing that would be?"

"Beats me." Lexy bit into the burger and then licked the ketchup that had oozed out of the side from her lip and started chewing.

"Did you get the door fixed?"

Lexy nodded, still chewing.

"And you didn't find anything missing?"

Lexy swallowed the bite of burger and went for a french fry. "Nope. The only thing I found was someone had messed with the cookbooks and recipes, but I don't think they took any of those either."

"Why do you think someone would do that?" Jack asked.

"I have no idea. The only thing I can figure is Caraleigh wanted my scone recipe, so she could make a batch and try to win the contest."

"You seem pretty sure it was this Caraleigh person."

Lexy felt a stab of panic. She couldn't tell Jack *why* she felt sure it was Caraleigh, because she couldn't tell him about the conversation she'd heard out by the dumpster. Not only would he frown on her dumpster-diving activities, but even worse, he'd know she'd lied to him about going out to dinner with Cassie and she didn't want him to lose trust in her.

"Well, I can't think of anyone else and her ring *was* there." Lexy shrugged then changed the subject. "Nans and the ladies wanted me to ask if you guys found out any more about the skull they dug up in the sewer."

"We didn't find anything," Jack said. "Those old sewer tunnels are a mess. Big sections have caved in and blocked off the entire tunnel. It's dangerous down there, which is why they are putting in new tunnels and blocking off the old ones. Those old tunnels could flood at any time and half the concrete would go with it."

"So that's it? You're not going to do any more investigating down there?"

Jack drained his glass of milk. "Nope. It's an old cold case and no one really cares about it, especially since we have so many current matters that need attention. Plus this whole bicentennial celebration is taking up a lot of our time. Which reminds me, I have to work the evening before and morning of the bicentennial. We're so shorthanded even we detectives have to pull a detail. But I'll be there in the afternoon to see you win a blue ribbon for your scones."

Lexy's heart swelled at his confidence in her as he cleared the empty dishes from the table, taking them to the trash and scraping before loading into the dishwasher. He turned to look at Lexy.

"I hope you and Nans don't have some harebrained idea about going down into the sewers to investigate the mystery of the skull," he said. "It's very dangerous down there and once they are done most of the old exits will be sealed off. Those old tunnels could fill up with water and you could be trapped in there."

Lexy could see genuine concern on Jack's face, but she felt her back stiffen. She *hated* anyone telling her what to do. Still, he did have a point.

"So, just where are the remaining entrances?" Lexy asked innocently.

"When they are done, the only manhole cover will be in the town center. But you can't open it, so don't get any ideas. It's too heavy—you need a special tool."

"Wait, I thought you said there were other entrances."

"There's supposed to be a few under the downtown area, but no one seems to know exactly where they are. The old records aren't that great," Jack said. "Then again, we didn't look too hard. And you shouldn't either."

"Of course not," Lexy said to appease Jack.

"That's my girl," Jack said.

Lexy smiled. Better to keep the peace now ... she was pretty sure she was going to do exactly as she pleased later on.

Feeling a change of subject was in order, she stood and grabbed Jack's hand. "Let's go over to our place. I have dessert."

Jack smiled, the glint in his eye telling Lexy his idea of dessert probably consisted of more than the frosted brownies she'd left on her counter.

"That's the best offer I've had all day," he said as he followed her out the door.

Chapter Eight

Lexy scowled out the window at the WOKQ van parked in front of *The Brew and Bake*, her fists clenched so tightly the nails bit into her palms.

So, the television station really is *doing a piece on the other bakery*, Lexy thought as she watched the camera crew unpack the van. Her heart sank when she compared the front room of *The Brew and Bake*, bustling with customers to her own empty one.

A movement on the sidewalk caught Lexy's eye. A customer? No, it was just the orange tiger cat that lived in Victor Nessbaum's antique store. He was an indoor cat, but sometimes he slipped out when the door was open. Lexy always tried to herd the cat back to Victor's whenever she saw him outside.

She stepped out onto the sidewalk, bending down to try to lure the cat over so she could pick him up and bring him back to Victor.

"Here, Kitty." She stuck out her hand to the cat who eyed her warily.

Behind her, she heard Victor's door open.

"Oh, that's where you are," Victor said to the cat. He pushed the door wide and gestured to the interior of the store. "Get back in here."

The cat turned, flicked his tail in Lexy's direction, and then trotted off into the store.

"He likes to get outside, but then doesn't know what to do with himself." Victor laughed. "Say, I'm glad I ran into you ... I sure would like to taste whatever it was you were baking yesterday afternoon. It smelled delicious in my store."

Lexy stood and crossed her arms over her chest. "Oh, you want to taste my baked goods and not those from across the street?"

Victor's brow creased and a sheepish look spread across his face. "Oh, did you see me over there? I was only trying out a sample so I could speak with authority when I said your pastries were the best."

Lexy thawed at the sincere look on the man's face. "Oh, okay, then ... come on over and you can try out my great-grandmother's famous scones. I made a slight variation to the recipe yesterday. That's what I was baking."

"Perfect. I'll just lock up." Victor reached inside his shop, grabbed his cane then flipped the lock on the door before closing it tight.

Lexy held her own door open while Victor shuffled down the walk, nodding to her as he stepped inside *The Cup and Cake*.

Behind the bakery case, Lexy pulled out the glass pedestal cake plate on which she'd arranged the scones and placed it on top of the case so Victor could get a better look.

"Which one do you want?" she asked.

"Hmm ..." Victor frowned at the pile, his eyes inspecting each scone. His brows furrowed and he rubbed his chin. "They all look so good."

His cane fell to the floor next to the case with a clatter and Lexy bent down to pick it up for him.

"Thanks," he said, then pointed to one of the scones on top. "I'll take that one."

Lexy smiled. "If you want, you can take a seat at the table and I'll bring it over along with some coffee or tea ... I'd love to know what you think of it."

"That would be wonderful." Victor turned and made his way to the self-serve station. "I can get my own tea."

Lexy put the scone on a small plate and took it over to the table where Victor sat with a steaming cup of tea in front of him. She slid into the chair across from him, eagerly watching the expression on his face as he took his first bite.

"This is delicious," he said chewing thoughtfully. "I particularly like the crumbly cinnamon and sugar top. You don't normally get that on a scone ... I think you have a winner here."

Thanks." Lexy beamed proudly as the bells over the door jingled to announce Nans, Ruth, Ida and Helen.

The four ladies greeted Lexy and Victor before marching purposely to one of the tables and slinging their purses over the backs of the chairs. Ruth gingerly placed several rolled up papers she'd carried in under her arm on the center of the table.

"What have you got there?" Victor asked.

"These are the blueprints for the old sewer system." Ruth unrolled one of them, spreading it on the table and holding down the ends with her hands while Nans, Ida and Helen rummaged in their purses for something to weight it down.

"You don't say?" Victor pushed his glasses up on his nose and leaned over for a better look at the print. "Where'd you get those?"

"Down at the town hall," Nans said producing a small stapler from her purse and plunking it down on one corner of the blueprint.

"Oh, I thought you had to wait ages to get those old prints run off down there." Victor returned his attention to his scone.

"Normally you do," Ida said placing the small rock she'd taken out of her purse on another corner of the print. "But it turns out someone had just recently gotten a copy of these, so Meredith had them right on her desk, waiting to put them away."

"'Course it helps to know someone down there." Helen threw down her purse and grabbed a stoneware mug from the self-serve coffee station, then placed it on the third corner of the blueprint.

"What do you plan to do with them?" Victor asked.

Ruth plunked her smartphone down on the last corner. "We're investigating the murder."

"Murder?" Victor's gray brows met his hairline.

"You know. The skull they found out there." Nans tilted her head toward the end of the street where the sewer work was still ongoing.

"I didn't realize there was an official murder investigation going on about that." Victor narrowed his eyes at Nans.

"Well, there isn't ... I mean not officially. The police don't seem interested in investigating. They said the murder was too long ago. But Ruth, Helen, Ida and I run our own detective agency, so we've taken it upon ourselves to find out the truth." Nans reached into her purse and pulled out a business card, which she handed to Victor.

Victor looked down at the card. "'Brook Ridge Falls Ladies Detective Club.' That's impressive ... and sounds like fun. Have you solved any good cases?"

Nans nodded. "We work with the police all the time and have helped them solve lots of cases. But, of course I can't be more specific due to confidentiality and all that."

"Of course, I understand," Victor said, "but what makes you so sure the person who belonged to the skull met with a suspicious death?"

Nans glanced at the others. "Well, we're not entirely sure, but we have it on good authority the skull had a bullet hole in it."

Victor gasped. "A bullet hole? Well, that sure does sound like foul play ... or maybe suicide."

"Either way, we need to investigate," Helen said. "He could have family members that have been wondering about him all these years."

"Of course." Victor slid his chair over next to Helen and bent his head over the blueprints. "So you're looking for a way into the old sewer system then?"

Ruth nodded. "We're hoping we can find some clues as to what happened back then."

"But how will you get in? I hear all the entrances are being sealed off with this new sewer project," Victor said.

"They are," Ida answered. "But we've learned there are some underground entrances and we plan to find out exactly where they are."

"Do you have any idea who the victim is?" Victor glanced at Helen out of the corner of his eye.

"None at all," Helen said. "We only know he's been down there for decades ... maybe sixty or seventy years even."

"Well, this sounds kind of dangerous," Victor said.

"And exciting," Nans added.

"It does sound rather exciting. An old buck like me could use some excitement. But you ladies could get hurt." Victor put his hand on Helen's arm. "Maybe I should accompany you."

"Maybe ..." Helen, Nans, Ruth and Ida exchanged uncertain glances. Lexy could tell they were torn between being polite and not wanting to let Victor in on their plans.

"I'm not sure," Nans said. "Lexy's the only one we ever let help us with our investigations."

"Perhaps we should take a look at these plans first," Victor suggested.

"Yes, let's." Helen re-anchored the corner that had come loose from under the mug and the five gray heads bent over the blueprint.

"This is the downtown section." Nans pointed to something on the upper left. "That's where the manhole cover for the main entrance is."

"Perfect, we'll just go in through there," Helen said.

"You can't," Lexy cut in and everyone turned to look at her. "Jack said it could only be opened with some special tool. It's too heavy for you and besides, it's right in the middle of downtown. What are you going to do? Stop the traffic so you can climb in the sewer hole?"

"We'll just have to find some other way," Nans said picking up one of the other rolls and spreading it on the table.

The five of them studied it for several minutes without finding an easy entrance to the sewer.

"There's nothing on this one, let's check the next one," Ruth said.

Victor looked at his watch. "Darn, I better get back to the store. I'm meeting a customer who wants to consign some vintage jewelry. You ladies will let me know if you need my assistance later on, won't you?"

The four ladies murmured a "Yes" and Victor stood, then nodded at each of them. Lexy thought she saw him wink at Helen, but she couldn't be sure.

He pulled his wallet out of his back pocket and turned to Lexy. "What do I owe you?"

"Oh, don't worry about that. It's on the house," Lexy said as she walked him to the door. "We neighbors have to stick together."

"Ain't that the truth?." Victor glanced knowingly across the street then headed out.

"I thought he'd never leave." Nans sighed.

"Yeah, imagine him trying to hone in on our investigation," Helen said.

"I think he's kind of sweet on you, Helen," Ida teased.

Helen's cheeks turned pink. "What? Don't be silly ... he's way too old for me."

Nans, Ruth and Ida raised their brows at her.

Helen looked at Lexy and smoothly changed the subject. "Did you ask Jack if the police found out anything about the murder when they were down in the sewer?"

"No, they didn't find anything and he made it sound like they aren't going to pursue it anymore," Lexy said.

"I figured that," Nans answered. "So it's up to us."

"Right." Lexy chewed her bottom lip. She wasn't sure how involved she wanted to get in this whole sewer business. Victor was right, it *did* seem dangerous. And the murder was decades old, so who really cared? But she didn't want to disappoint Nans and she knew the older woman would go ahead no matter what. Lexy knew she couldn't talk Nans out of it. Her only hope was that Nans would get too busy with the historical society project to have time to investigate.

"I did find something in Jack's basement you guys might be interested in," Lexy said.

"Really?" Nans raised a brow at Lexy.

"Yeah, he had a stack of newspapers from 1948 down there. I saved them out for you guys."

"Oh, that's wonderful ... does it have articles from the bank robbery?" Ida asked.

"I don't know. I didn't read any of them."

"Let's see them." Ruth looked around the shop. "Where are they?"

"Sorry, I left them at Jack's," Lexy said. "But I promise to pick them up tonight and bring them to work tomorrow, so if you guys are going to stop by, I'll have them."

"We'll make a point of it, won't we, girls?" Ida asked.

"Of course," Nans answered and then turned to Lexy. "Now let's get back to these sewer plans, I don't see any entrances we can use on either of these."

The ladies rolled out the rest of the sheets and poured over them. Finally, Nans said, "I don't think we have the whole town here."

Lexy frowned down at the papers. "It sure looks like it."

"No," Nans insisted. "Look. Here is Adams Street, then Berkley, then Maple, but it ends at Cedar. This section of town here is missing."

"Hmmm ... You're right," Ida said.

"Wait. Let's lay them out end to end." Lexy grabbed the papers to do just that when the bell over the door jingled and Lexy turned to see a middle-aged man enter the bakery.

A customer!

She dropped the papers, a smile springing to her lips as she made her way behind the bakery case from which, hopefully, the customer would be making some purchases.

"Can I help you?" she asked.

"Why yes, I'd like one of these scones, if I may." The man pointed to the glass pedestal and Lexy grabbed a square of waxed paper and selected the largest scone.

"Is that to eat here?" Lexy asked.

"Yes."

"We have coffee and tea over at the self-serve station if you'd like," she offered.

The man looked over as he pulled out his wallet. "I'll take a large coffee too."

Lexy rang up the purchase and the man ambled over to pour himself a coffee while Nans, Ruth, Ida, and Helen moved the papers that were spilling over onto the other tables.

The man took a seat and the ladies bent back over the blueprints talking in hushed tones. Lexy busied herself cleaning off the self-serve station.

"Aghh ... pfft."

Lexy whirled around to see the man grabbing at his tongue while making choking and gurgling noises.

"Are you okay? What happened?" Lexy rushed to his side.

"Okay? Pfftt ..." The man glared at Lexy as he continued to grab at his tongue. "I should say not!"

Nans, Ruth, Ida and Helen had stopped talking and were staring at the man.

Lexy raised her brows at him. "I don't understand, what's the matter?"

"I'll tell you what the matter is," he said stabbing his finger at the half-eaten pastry. "There's a big clump of hair in my scone!"

Chapter Nine

"What?" Lexy stared at the scone. "I can assure you there are no hairs in my pastries!"

"You can see it right there," the man sputtered as he slammed closed the notebook he had open on the table beside him.

Lexy bent down to look closer at the scone and gasped. There *was* some hair there ... a small clump of short light-colored hairs.

"What's this? These weren't here before," Lexy said.

Nans, Ruth, Ida and Helen craned their necks to see the hairs.

"Oh dear, that does look like hair," Ida said.

"But how would it get there?" Lexy asked. "I have a very clean kitchen."

"That's right, she's never had any kind of problem with contamination before," Nans added.

Lexy narrowed her eyes at the man who hastily jammed his arms in the sleeves of his coat. "Wait a minute, how do I know you didn't plant that in there?"

The man's faced turned red. "Plant it? Madam, don't you know who I am?"

Lexy glanced at Nans and the ladies who all shook their heads. "No."

"I'm Edgar Royce," the man stated.

Nans gasped.

"The food critic?" Lexy's brows shot upwards. That would be terribly bad luck to have one of the most influential food critics find a hair in her scone—the very recipe she was planning to enter in the bicentennial contest.

The man nodded. "And you can rest assured I will *not* be giving you a favorable review. In fact, I should probably call the health inspector on you."

Lexy's stomach twisted. That was the last thing she needed on top of everything else. The timing of this was unfortunate ... too unfortunate not to be suspicious.

"Wait a minute," she said as the man brushed past her on his way to the door. "What made you decide to come here today?"

"I got a call. Someone raving about your pastries and saying I should try the scones since it was some famous family recipe or something," he said. "I thought it would make an appealing article as I was told your great-grandmother won contests with that same recipe. I can only assume she omitted the hair."

"Do you know who called?" Lexy followed him to the door. "A man or a woman?"

"Lady, I have no idea. I just got the message from my editor." He stepped around her toward the door. "Now, if you'll excuse me, I'll be on my way."

"Of course," Lexy said. "At least let me give you your money back. I'm so sorry this happened."

"Never mind about the money. If you want my advice, I think you better go over your kitchen with a fine tooth comb and make sure you have sanitary baking practices," he barked before turning on his heel and storming out the door.

"Well, I never!" Ruth said. "What was that all about?"

"It appears as if someone is setting me up." Lexy slid her eyes toward *The Brew and Bake*. "And I think I have a pretty good idea who it is."

***

The cold air stung Lexy's face as she flung open the door to *The Cup and Cake*. She didn't notice it though, despite the fact she hadn't put on a coat. Her anger kept her warm.

She stormed across the street, past the television crew loading their equipment into the van, and straight into *The Brew and Bake*.

"Just what are you up to?" she demanded.

Caraleigh looked at her in surprise. "Excuse me? Are you referring to the television segment?"

"No. I'm referring to Edgar Royce."

Caraleigh answered her with a blank stare. The customers who had been in the shop, probably trying to get their fifteen minutes of fame on television, edged their way to the door.

"Don't play dumb with me." Lexy stepped closer to the blonde baker. "You know who he is—the food critic."

Caraleigh fisted her hands on her hips. "I have no idea what you are talking about and I don't appreciate your tone."

Lexy got right in Caraleigh's face. "Don't give me that. I know you sabotaged my scones and then sent him in to give me a bad review."

"Like you should talk. What about the article in the Sentinel bashing my pastries? Wasn't it written by one of your friends sitting in your bakery right now?"

Caraleigh shot her arm out to point across the street. Lexy's gaze followed noticing Nans, Ruth,

Ida and Helen, their faces pressed against the glass window of *The Cup and Cake* looking back at them.

"She did an independent test comparing them!" Lexy said.

Caraleigh's face started to turn an unhealthy shade of pink. "Independent my ass. First you accuse me of being a thief, and now this? You better watch it or you might find yourself on the business end of a lawsuit."

Anger bubbled up inside Lexy. She jabbed her finger in Caraleigh's face. "*You* sue *me*? Ha! That's a laugh. I'm the one that should sue you!"

"Okay, break it up."

Lexy whipped her head around to see Watson Davies quickly making her way toward them.

"What is it with you two?" Davies pushed the two of them apart glaring at each of them in turn.

"She's trying to ruin my business," Lexy complained to Davies.

"No! *She's* trying to ruin *mine*!" Caraleigh said.

"You sound like two year olds," Davies replied.

Caraleigh's brows dipped. "What are *you* doing here, anyway?"

"I was actually on my way to *The Cup and Cake* to talk to Lexy about the break-in and I saw the two of you fighting over here."

"So, you checked out her alibi?" Lexy thrust her chin toward Caraleigh. "Are you going to arrest her?"

"No. Her alibi checked out just like she said."

Lexy's stomach sank. "What? Well, surely you're not going to believe her brother. He probably lied for her. I mean it *must* have been her—who else would break in?"

"That's what I wanted to talk to you about." Davies took Lexy's elbow and tugged her toward the door. "It would be better if we talked over in your store, though."

"See ... I told you I didn't do it!" Caraleigh yelled after them. "Hey, I want my ring back and I might want to press ch—"

Davies closed the door, cutting off Caraleigh's rant. She kept her vise-like grip on Lexy's elbow, propelling her across the street and into *The Cup and Cake*.

Nans, Ruth, Ida and Helen, who had watched them intently as they crossed the street, sat facing the door with questioning looks.

"Well, did she do it? Nans asked.

"She denied it, but it *must* have been her," Lexy replied.

"What are you guys talking about?" Davies forehead creased at Lexy.

"A food critic found hair in Lexy's scones ... so naturally, we assumed that *other* woman planted it." Nans gestured to the scone on the table, one small bite taken out of the corner.

Davies looked at the plate. "It does have hair on it. But how would she plant it? Was she over here?"

Nans pressed her lips together. "I didn't see her. *Was* she here Lexy?"

Lexy frowned. "No ... but it must have been her."

"Maybe it was just an unhappy coincidence," Ruth offered.

"Is that what you were arguing about?" Davies asked Lexy.

"Yes. She's been out to get me since she opened." Lexy felt her anger rising again. "I mean just look at how she made her bakery the same colors and design as mine ... the sign is almost same and she's been undercutting my prices! It just *had* to have been her that broke in! And can you believe she had the nerve to accuse *me* of trying to ruin *her* business?"

"The casual observer might see it that way," Davies pointed out.

"What? Are you saying you think *I'm* behind all this?" Lexy asked incredulously.

Davies held her hand up to ward off Lexy's anger. "I said the *casual* observer. If you think about it logically, you have a solid motive because her business is a threat to yours. So, since she has an alibi for the break-in, I should probably get one from you, too."

"You seriously don't think I broke into my own bakery, do you?" Lexy fumed.

"No, but it won't hurt for you to prove you couldn't have." Davies whipped out her cell phone and poised her fingertips over the keypad. "So where were you that night?"

"Well, I'm sure I was home with Jack. No, wait. That was two nights ago? I went out with Cassie after work, then home with Jack."

"Okay, great. Where did you go with Cassie? A restaurant or bar? Did anyone see you?"

Lexy's top teeth worried her bottom lip. She was starting to regret the dumpster dive—now she was getting even deeper into the lie and that was never a good thing.

"We went to *The Glenview* for dinner." Lexy grimaced at the high pitch of her voice. She'd have to remember to get her story straight with Cassie. Of course, she probably *should* come clean about where they really were, but that would make her look guilty for sure. "We didn't see anyone we know there though."

"Did you pay with a credit card? We could verify it that way."

"No, we paid in cash." Lexy absently wiped her sweaty palms on her jeans.

Davies sighed. "Okay, well that doesn't give me much to go on, but at least I can find out when you got home from Jack. If only I could narrow down what time the break-in happened, that would make it so much easier."

"I can't believe *my* shop was broken in to and now *I'm* the suspect," Lexy said.

"You're not a suspect," Davies answered. "I'm just covering all the angles. You must admit you do seem to have quite the adversarial relationship with Ms. Brewster."

"Well, she's not very easy to get along with," Lexy said.

"Yeah, I know." Davies slid her gaze across the street. "She got on my bad side too, remember? Honestly, I would be happy to discover it *was* her, but I have to work with the facts."

"Right. Sorry. I guess this sewer business has me all worked up." Lexy gestured toward the torn up sidewalk. "No one can even get to my shop and she's getting all the business."

"Hang in there. The sewer work should be all tied up the day after tomorrow. I hear they have a mandate to finish it before the practice parade on Friday night." Davies made to leave, reached for the doorknob, then turned back. "If you think of anything else that might shed light on the robbery, let me know."

With a jingle of the bells over the door, the detective disappeared out onto the street.

"Well that sure is strange," Nans said.

"What? That her alibi checks out?" Lexy asked.

"Yes. Did you ever think maybe it *isn't* her doing all this?"

Lexy shook her head. "That doesn't make any sense. It *has* to be her. I found her ring right in the pile of recipes!"

"Lexy's right," Ida chimed in. "She has a strong motive. Besides if it's not her, who else would go to all this trouble … and why?"

Chapter Ten

The next day, Lexy got to the bakery early to work on another variation of the scone recipe. She avoided the morning paper because she didn't want to see the review from Edgar Royce.

The morning had been productive with Cassie helping her to bake a batch of cupcakes, chocolate cream pies and Snickerdoodles in-between waiting on customers and chatting. They were just now getting around to trying out the scone recipe variation.

"I don't know how she could have tampered with that scone," Cassie said as she rolled dough onto the marble counter.

"I know. None of the other scones had hair on them. It's just so strange." Lexy broke and separated an egg, expertly pouring the white into a small bowl, then added a dash of cream and started beating it with a fork. "Unless she broke in. The scones were sitting out in the case all night."

Cassie cut the dough carefully into triangles. "But the bakery was locked up tight as a drum the next morning, right? How would she pick the right piece to sabotage, anyway?"

"I know. Only one piece had the hair on it." Lexy brushed the egg white mixture over each triangle of dough then sprinkled a cinnamon and sugar mixture on top.

"It's strange that the contaminated piece ended up being the exact piece you gave Edgar Royce."

"Very." An image of Victor's cat came to mind. Had she been petting the cat before or after she served Edgar? Was it possible the cat hair had been on her sleeve and she had actually been the one to contaminate the piece?

Lexy's stomach twisted—it couldn't be. She tried to be so careful about stuff like that. "Maybe someone paid him off to plant it himself?"

Cassie scrunched up her face. "I doubt it. I don't think someone like him would take a payoff. People like that have to work too hard to build up their reputation."

"True." Lexy said as Cassie picked up the pan with the scones and headed to the oven.

"Oh, and one other thing," Lexy said. "We need to get our stories straight about the night of the break-in. Davies asked where I was. I told her that you and I were at *The Glenview*. Just in case she asks."

Cassie cocked an eyebrow at Lexy. "Jeez, now you want me to lie to the police?"

Lexy flushed. "Well, we can't very well tell her we were hanging around Caraleigh's dumpster!"

"I know. No problem. I have lots of practice lying to the police."

Lexy laughed. Cassie had always been a bit on the wild side and never trusted anyone in authority, including the police. In their younger days, she'd been in quite a few scrapes, which had necessitated not being truthful to law enforcement on several occasions. The irony of Cassie being happily married to a police detective now was not lost on Lexy.

The bell on the front door jingled. To Lexy's delight, the day had brought a slow but steady trickle of customers and she and Cassie had taken turns waiting on them. It was Lexy's turn now. She peeled off the clear, thin food service gloves she'd worn to apply the cinnamon mixture and tossed them in the trash as she headed to the front of the bakery.

Nans, Ruth, Ida and Helen looked up from where they stood in front of the bakery case.

"Morning Lexy," they said in unison.

"Morning ladies. What can I get you?"

"Do we dare try the scones?" Ida twittered and then blanched at Lexy's withering look. "Sorry dear, of course we'll have a scone. Make that two scones each—we'll take the second one home with us."

Lexy dished out the scones while the women helped themselves to coffee from the self-serve station. They settled into their favorite table with a large pile of napkins. Lexy watched in amusement as each of them unfolded one large napkin, placed a scone in the middle, then folded the edges around the scone to wrap it in a tight package they then shoved into their giant patent leather purses.

Placing the purses on the backs of their chairs, they dug into the scones on the plates in front of them.

"Lexy, did you remember those newspapers from Jack's?" Nans asked.

"Yes, I have them right here." Lexy picked the stack of yellowed papers from the corner and brought them over to the table.

"Oh, there's quite a lot of them," Nans said.

"I think the whole year is here." Ruth pushed her plate aside and pulled the stack of papers in front of her. She divided the stack into four equal piles, then handed each lady a pile, keeping one for herself.

Each unfolded her paper carefully and set about looking through it in between nibbles of scone and sips of coffee.

"Look at these ads for hats!" Nans angled her paper so everyone could see the black and white drawings of 1940s style women's hats.

"Imagine having to wear a fancy hat every day," Ida twittered.

"I know!" Helen said. "Back then people did dress much nicer, though."

"Yep. Every day clothing back then would be considered formal now. Women in dresses, men in suits. It was the norm back then." Ruth held up her paper showing an old black and white photograph of downtown Brook Ridge Falls with people dressed in 1940s fashions.

"Hold on girls." Ida grabbed onto Nans' arm. "I think I've hit the mother lode."

Lexy and the three other ladies turned questioning looks on her. She slid the paper toward them. "This issue is full of articles on the 1948 robbery!"

"Let me see." Nans reached over toward the paper. "Are there any photographs of the gangsters?"

"Yeah. Pictures of the perps would sure liven up our display," Ruth said.

"Yes! Here's one of Midas Mulcahey." Ida laid the paper flat on the table, tapping her index finger on the faded picture of a man.

Lexy squinted down at the picture. "That's pretty faded. You can barely make him out."

"Wait a minute." The tone of Nans' voice made Lexy's stomach tighten. "Is *that* what I think it is?"

Ida dug a large magnifying glass out of her purse and placed it over the picture. Four gray heads bent down to look through the glass.

"It is!" Nans said. "Midas Mulcahey had two gold front teeth—just like the skull they dug up from the sewer."

Chapter Eleven

Lexy stared wide-eyed at Nans. "You think that skull is the gangster Midas Mulcahey?"

"Sure." Nans nodded. "How many people do you know who have two gold teeth? Says right here those teeth are what gave him the nickname Midas."

Ida glanced out the window. "I wonder how long he's been down there."

"According to what we've read in the research, he disappeared right after the bank robbery," Ruth said. "I just assumed he ran off somewhere to spend the money."

"Yeah, I bet everyone did." Lexy followed Ida's gaze.

"But he was here in town the whole time," Helen said.

"Do you think he hid the money down in the sewers?" Cassie had come out from the back room just in time to overhear the news about Midas.

"I can't think of a better place to hide it," Nans said.

"I bet someone killed him for it! Probably one of the other gangsters." Ida stabbed her finger toward the article in the paper that named the alleged bank robbers.

"Boots Bennett and someone named The Bomb," Lexy said. "Seems like it would be hard to track them down with just those nick-names to go on."

"And don't forget about the woman … Rose somebody," Ruth added.

"If we could track them down, we might be able to learn what happened." Nans pressed her lips together. "One of them is probably the killer."

"And they probably took off with all the loot," Helen added.

"We don't know that for sure." Ida's eyes sparkled with excitement. "The money could still be down there."

"Either way, now there's even more of a reason for us to go down in the old sewer system," Nans said.

"That's right." Ruth shoved the newspapers aside, bent down and picked up the rolled up sewer plans from where she had put them next to her chair. "We can solve the mystery of the robbery, find out what happened to Midas, and maybe even recover the stolen money!"

"Yes, there might still be a reward to recover it." Nans lowered her voice to a whisper. "So let's not tell anyone what we've discovered."

"Not a soul," Ruth said. The others nodded in agreement and crossed their hearts as they folded up the old newspapers, put them in a tidy pile in the corner and covered them with their coats.

"Teddy Mokewitz told me that, in addition to the manhole covers, some of the old mill buildings had access to the sewer channels." Helen pushed her glasses up on her nose. "So we should be aware of that while reviewing these plans."

"Oh, darn. Here comes that Victor guy again." Ida frowned out the window.

"Probably coming over to see Helen." Nans giggled.

Helen scowled at Nans.

"Remember, don't tell him about the newspapers," Ruth whispered as the door jingled open.

Victor looked around the bakery, his face lighting up as his eyes came to rest on Nans and the ladies at their usual table. "I see my favorite girls are here."

The ladies, polite as ever, smiled and nodded.

"Hi Victor," Cassie said. "Here for your morning muffin?"

Victor smiled. "Yes. Do you have any blueberry today?"

"Of course." Cassie got behind one of the bakery cases and took out a tray loaded with muffins. "Any muffin in particular?"

"No, you pick," Victor answered from the coffee station where he was pouring a hazelnut coffee into one of the to-go cups. He paid, took the muffin from Cassie and then came over to the table where, much to the obvious dismay of the ladies, he pulled a seat up next to Helen.

"I see you are you still going over those sewer plans," he said taking a sip from the paper coffee cup.

"Oh, we're just fooling around," Nans said. "We really can't go down in there. It wouldn't be prudent; especially at our age. Isn't that right girls?"

Ida, Helen and Ruth nodded.

Victor narrowed his eyes at Nans. "Really? I thought you girls were the adventurous types what with your detective agency and all."

"We prefer to do our detecting on the computer and on paper." Nans pointed to the blueprints. "We rarely go out in the field."

"I see." Victor turned to Lexy. "Did I see you having another run-in with the *other* baker?"

Lexy looked across the street. Just the thought of the *other* baker was enough to make her blood boil. She took a deep breath, willing herself to remain calm. "Yes I did. I think she is trying to sabotage me."

"Why do you say that?" Victor's voice rose as he spoke and Lexy thought she heard a hint of something. Alarm? Concern? She wasn't sure which.

"Edgar Royce, the food critic, was in here yesterday and somehow he got a contaminated scone. I just know she was behind it."

Victor nodded. "She's not to be trusted. She's doing something suspicious over there. Can't you get your new husband to investigate or shut her down?"

Lexy wished she could. The truth was, Jack didn't seem to be interested in what the other bakery was doing or why they were doing it. Besides, he was too honest to play favorites.

"If only. But don't worry. I'm sure the police will figure out what she's up to." Lexy wished she felt as confident as she sounded.

"Well I hope so—we don't need the likes of her messing things up here." Victor stood. "My offer is still open. If you ladies decide to venture into the sewer, or go on any other type of adventure, I would love to accompany you."

"Thanks. We'll keep you in mind." Nans plastered a smile on her face as Victor turned to leave.

"Phew, I was afraid he was going to stay all afternoon," Ida said as soon as he was out the door.

"Me too," Helen added. "I wish he would stop offering to come with us as if we need a man around. We can certainly handle a little sewer excursion all on our own."

"Of course we can!" Nans said.

"Right on," Ida added.

"Men!" This from Ruth who stood to bend over the blueprints.

Lexy admired the old ladies' spunk, but she had to admit she didn't share their confidence about going down in the sewer. The odds were slim the money was still down there and it could be dangerous. Jack had said the whole thing could flood or crumble. Any clues to the decades-old robbery were probably long gone, anyway. She hoped they didn't find another access into the sewer. If they did, she'd have to come up with some way to talk them out of going in.

"You were right yesterday, Mona," Ruth said to Nans. "There *was* one section of blueprint missing."

"I knew it!" Nans' triumph was short-lived. "But that means we won't be able to look everywhere. It would be just our luck the entrance we need is on the missing blueprint."

"Well, then you're going to owe me something extra in my Christmas stocking." Ruth's eyes twinkled as she reached under her chair. "Because I went down to the town hall earlier today and got the missing blueprint."

"They had it?" Nans asked.

"Well, not the actual print. Meredith ran this one off from a microfiche picture," Ruth answered. "It's rather strange. She thinks the last person to look at the hard copy of blueprints stole that page."

Lexy's forehead creased. "Why would anyone do that?"

Ruth shrugged. "Beats me."

Nans straightened in her chair. "Isn't it obvious? They didn't want anyone else to see what was on the blueprint."

"Why not?" Helen paused, holding the scone halfway to her mouth.

"Because they're onto the bank robbery loot, same as we are."

Ida gasped. "You mean we have competition?"

"It would seem that way," Nans replied.

"But who?" Helen asked. "Who else could have possibly figured this out?"

Nans shrugged. "Anyone who saw them pull the skull up and knew about Midas Mulcahey."

"Well, I wouldn't think too many people would know about something that happened so long ago," Helen said.

"Sure, but it only takes one person. Someone on the police investigation or someone in the historical society that knows the history," Nans suggested.

"Oh, wait." Ruth grabbed her purse from the back of the chair and set it in her lap. "They have a card you sign to view the blueprints just like when you take out books at the library. I have it here since I signed out the other blueprints. Let me see …"

Lexy held her breath as Ruth pulled several objects out of her purse, placing them on the table and diving back in until she finally retrieved a small card.

Squinting down at it, she adjusted her glasses. "Yes, here it is. The last person to take these out was someone named Brewster ... Caraleigh Brewster."

***

Lexy gasped, her head jerking up to look at the bakery across the street.

"What's the matter, dear? Do you know this person?" Ruth asked.

"I can't believe it ... Caraleigh Brewster is the baker across the street." Lexy shot her arm out pointing toward the bakery, and four gray heads turned to look out the window.

"You don't say," Ida said.

"Why would a baker want to get in the sewer?" Helen asked.

"I have no idea," Lexy said, her eyes riveted on the other bakery. Inside, Caraleigh swiped at her cafe tables with a white towel. Lexy took little consolation in the fact *The Brew and Bake* was as empty as her own bakery.

"Well, it's simple," Nans said matter-of-factly. "She must know about the treasure."

"How would she know?" Ida asked.

"Who knows? Isn't she new in town?" Nans looked up at Lexy. "What do you know about her?"

"Nothing, really. She was getting the bakery ready to open right before I left on my honeymoon. When I came back it was in full swing."

"A suspicious bakery that sells grocery store baked goods." Nans narrowed her eyes and looked out the window. "She probably doesn't even know how to bake."

"Oh, come on, Mona." Ruth raised her brows at Nans. "Why would someone who doesn't know how to bake open a bakery?"

"I know why," Ida cut in. "It's a cover!"

Ruth's eyes narrowed, she tapped her index finger on her pursed lips. "You mean somehow she found out about the robbery and thinks the treasure is still here in town, so she came here to ferret it out. Maybe she knew all about Midas Mulcahey and recognized the teeth in the skull, then went to get the blueprints, planning on getting into the sewer just like we did."

"But she was here before they even found the skull," Lexy said. "And why would she go to all the trouble of opening a bakery and then try to drive me out of business?"

"Yeah, why break in *here*? Why sabotage your scones?" Helen added.

"It doesn't make any sense." Lexy spread her arms and let them slap back to her sides.

"Wait a minute ..." Nans bent closely over the table, her index finger tracing the lines on the blueprint. "Let's see ... this is Main Street and here is the intersection of Duvall and Main. Then it branches off to Elm and ... Yep, just as I thought!"

Nans straightened up and looked at the group, her green eyes sparkling with enthusiasm.

"What?" Lexy squinted at her grandmother.

Nans pointed at the table. "If this blueprint is correct, the underground access to the sewers is right below your bakery."

Chapter Twelve

Lexy's stomach twisted as she stared down at the blueprint.

"Below the bakery? I don't get it." Lexy remembered the conversation she and Cassie overheard behind Caraleigh's dumpster. The other baker had said they had to "figure out a way to get *access* across the street." Lexy had *thought* they meant into the bakery, but what if they were talking about the sewer access *under* the bakery? And if so, why did they break in and mess around with the recipes?

Lexy didn't have time to think about it, because Nans, Ruth, Ida and Helen had already jumped up out of their seats and were making a beeline for the door to the basement.

Lexy hurried after them, passing a confused looking Cassie who had poked her head out of the kitchen at the commotion.

"Can you watch the front? We need to check something out downstairs," Lexy yelled on her way past. "I'll fill you in later."

"Sure, no problem." Cassie's voice followed Lexy around the corner where the door to the basement had been flung open.

Lexy stepped on the top stair, then stopped and peered down into the dark basement where she could hear the four ladies chattering on the stairs below her.

"Is there a light switch down here? I can't see my hand in front of my face."

"Does anyone have a flashlight?"

"I do, but it's in my purse upstairs!"

Lexy felt along the wall tentatively, relieved when her hands met the hard plastic of the light switch instead of something less desirable ... like a spider. She flipped the switch and a dull yellow light illuminated the basement below.

Nans looked up at her. "Oh thanks, dear."

Lexy descended the rest of the stairs, the smell of mildew tickling her nose and causing her to stifle a sneeze.

"Have you ever noticed a door or manhole cover or anything down here?" Nans asked.

Lexy looked around. She'd only been down here a couple of times. She found it a bit creepy and too musty to store any of her ingredients. The hard concrete floor was dirty and scuffed with age. The brick walls were dark, the mortar falling out in chunks here and there. It was filled with old shelves and metal ducts and pipes from the previous resident.

"I never really looked down here," she admitted.

"Where should we start?" Ida turned around in the middle of the basement, looking for a good starting point.

"What are we even looking for?" Ruth asked. "A door? A manhole cover?"

"I'm not sure," Nans replied. "But it makes sense that whatever it is would be over near the street. That's where the sewer tunnels are."

"That wall over there is the one that faces the street." Lexy pointed to a wall covered in floor to ceiling metal shelving to her left.

Nans walked over to inspect it. She ran her finger across one of the shelves, stirring up a cloud of dust. "We'll need to remove these shelving units so we can see the actual wall of the building.

Ida tugged on a corner. It didn't budge. "They're nailed in."

"We'll need to get some tools," Ruth said.

"And our work clothes," Helen added.

"And maybe even hard hats." Ida looked warily at the unsteady shelves.

"I don't get it," Lexy said. "What does this have to do with Caraleigh sabotaging my food, stealing recipes, lowballing my prices and having television spots?"

"Isn't it obvious?" Nans asked.

"No." Lexy gave an exasperated shrug and held her hands up.

"She was trying to put you out of business so she could rent this space. That way she'd be free to come down and explore the sewer for the money without anyone knowing."

"So, her whole bakery is a scam? A ruse to get into this basement?"

"I think so." Nans tilted her head and looked thoughtful. "She must have known about this before they found the skull. That's the real reason she came to Brook Ridge Falls. And if the skull didn't show up, she would have been able to take her sweet time poking around in the sewer until she found the money, because no one else would have suspected it might be in there."

"Right," Ida added. "She must have found out about it some other way and come to town specifically to get into the sewers. I bet she got those plans when she first arrived in town. Maybe even before she opened the bakery."

"Seems like an awful lot of trouble to go to just on the off-chance there's a treasure in there," Lexy said.

"That's just it," Nans said. "She must *know* the treasure is there for sure.

"Which means we need to get in there fast ... *before* she does," Ida added.

"Not only that, but now that the skull has surfaced and the sewer is being closed off, she's sure to know she'll have to step up her efforts to get to the treasure before someone else does or the access to the sewers is blocked off," Nans said. "Which means Lexy better be extra careful because, if my guess is right, this Caraleigh person will likely stop at nothing to get in here."

***

"Let me get this straight ... There's a secret access to the sewers right in our basement and Caraleigh is doing all this to get in there?" Cassie eyed Lexy doubtfully.

Lexy had to admit, it did sound rather far-fetched, but it was the only explanation that made sense. And the more Lexy thought about it, the more sense it made.

"I know it sounds crazy, but the money from the robbery could be sitting down there." Lexy looked out the window toward *The Brew and Bake*. Was Caraleigh looking out her window toward *them*? Had she guessed they'd discovered the secret sewer entrance? And if she had, what would she do?

"Well, I guess it might be worth a million dollars to go to all that trouble," Cassie said. "Still, seems like there would be an easier way to get into those sewers."

"There isn't," Lexy explained. "Believe me, we've looked. Anyway, Nans and the ladies are going to be back soon with the tools and we'll close up and get to work downstairs. Do you want to stay and help?"

"I'd love to, but John made plans for dinner with his parents tonight." Cassie made a face.

Lexy laughed. Cassie and her in-laws didn't exactly get along, but she made the effort for John's sake.

Lexy looked at her watch. "It's almost quitting time, so why don't you go ahead and take off. I'm sure you can use the extra time to meditate or something so you have a calm demeanor for dinner."

"Thanks." Cassie untied her apron and hung it on the hook, then picked up her coat. "I was thinking more like some pre-dinner cocktails."

Lexy watched Cassie go out the back just as the bells over the door tinkled and Nans, Ruth, Ida and Helen came in the front. They had their usual large old-lady purses and Nans and Ruth were each holding the handle of a duffel bag that hung between them.

"We brought the tools," Nans said as they shrugged out of their coats to reveal dirty, stained tee shirts and sweat pants. Ida pulled a pair of leather work gloves out of her purse and put them on. Helen tied a bandana around her head. Nans and Ruth dropped the heavy duffel bag and each took a chair.

"I'll just close up shop." Lexy made her way to the door, all the while stealing inconspicuous glances at *The Brew and Bake*. She could have sworn the other baker was watching her as she flipped the sign to "Closed".

Nans motioned for her to turn off the light and she did. Dusk had fallen and the streetlight outside had just flickered on, leaving the inside of *The Cup and Cake* in shadows.

Nans leaned toward the rest of them, her voice lowered to a whisper. "Okay, now I want to make sure you're all aware of the danger and everyone is on board no matter what happens."

The three other ladies nodded and murmured their agreement.

"Lexy, are you in?" Nans asked.

"Damn right I'm in," Lexy said. "I have a bigger stake than anyone here, and hopefully whatever we find will either make Caraleigh pack up and go home, or prove what she's really up to. But I need some hard evidence before I call Davies … Maybe we'll find what I need to get rid of Caraleigh down there."

"Alrighty then…" Nans pulled a baseball cap out of her purse and stuffed it on her head, then picked up one handle of the duffel bag. "…let's go!"

Lexy followed the ladies down into the basement where they set the duffel bag on the floor in front of the shelving. Nans bent over the bag and pulled out a sledgehammer. Ruth reached in and came up with a crowbar. Ida found a tire iron and Helen a hacksaw.

The shelving had been nailed into the brick and they started in the corner with Ruth sticking the edge of the crowbar in and Nans banging on it. Once it had pulled out from the wall, Ida added her muscle by sticking the tire iron in and Ruth tried to saw the giant nail apart with the hacksaw.

They pushed, pulled, pounded and sawed until finally the shelf crashed to the floor, revealing the wall of bricks behind it. Lexy thought she heard a distraught mew come from somewhere next door.

"There's nothing here but a brick wall." Ida's disappointment was obvious.

"Oh don't worry," Nans said cheerfully. "There's plenty more wall. She moved to the next shelf and started the process all over again. Then the next. Lexy's spirits were starting to sink dismally by the time they got to the fourth shelf.

"I'm not sure there's anything here." Lexy picked a cobweb out of her hair. "Maybe those old blueprints are wrong."

"Nonsense." Nans raised her arms over her head and brought the sledgehammer down on the end of the crowbar. "We're not stopping until we've dislodged every shelf unit. There's only two more to go."

Ruth jammed the crowbar behind the shelf unit and pried it away.

"Look!" Ruth pointed excitedly behind the shelf.

Nans, Ida, Helen and Lexy ran up behind her, jockeying for position so they could see behind the shelf. Lexy's heart lurched when she saw what Ruth had been excited about.

An old wooden door.

The ladies worked on the shelf with a burst of energy and it crashed to the floor, revealing an old oak door set into the brick wall. In the middle of the door sat a wide plank, which dropped into metal brackets on either side of the door, presumably to keep it from being pushed open from the sewer side.

Lexy and Nans raced to one side of the plank, Ida and Ruth to the other.

"Ready?" Helen asked. "On the count of three ... One ... Two ... Three ..."

The four women pushed the heavy plank up and out of the brackets. It clattered to the floor revealing a large iron door handle.

Nans rubbed her hands together. "This is it, girls."

She reached out and tugged at the handle.

Nothing.

Planting her feet firmly in front of the door, she grabbed the handle again and leaned back.

The door did not budge.

"Let me do that." Ida pushed Nans out of the way and tried opening the door, but it remained firmly shut.

"Hold on you guys, I'll do it." Lexy pushed Ida out of the way and took her turn.

The door did not open.

"It's locked," Lexy said, her heart sinking.

"Locked? Now doesn't that figure? We finally uncover the door and it's locked," Ruth said.

"Can't you guys pick the lock?" Lexy asked. She knew at least one of the ladies had skills in the lock-picking area.

Ruth bent down to inspect the handle, or rather the keyhole, underneath. It was the type that took an old skeleton key—a gigantic skeleton key judging by the size. "No can do. This lock is too big. We need a key."

"Maybe the key is in here." Lexy looked around the basement, picking up some scraps that lay in piles looking for the key.

"It's probably long gone," Nans said. "But I think I know where we can get a skeleton key that just might fit.

"Where?" Four heads turned to look at Nans.

"Victor's antique shop."

Chapter Thirteen

Lexy almost told Jack about the secret door, but she knew he'd give her a hard time about going into the sewer. Maybe he'd even get the police involved. She couldn't risk them screwing everything up, so she'd managed to keep mum about it all night. Needless to say, she was glad when morning came and she could escape to the bakery.

Walking in through the back, she glanced toward the basement door, her stomach taut with excited anticipation. She couldn't wait to get down there and open the door, but Victor's shop had been closed last night so they hadn't been able to get a key. Not only that, but she still had a bakery to run and had a ton of things to do, not the least of which was trying one last tweak to the scone recipe. Tomorrow was the bicentennial celebration and she'd need to have the recipe perfected by morning in order to bake a fresh batch in time for the judging.

Nans, Ruth, Ida and Helen had some finishing touches to do on their display for the historical society, so, even though they all were dying to get into the sewer, they'd decided it was best to meet later in the afternoon, get the key from Victor and then get into the sewer once Lexy closed the shop for the day.

"I could have sworn I saw Caraleigh Brewster looking over here with binoculars when I drove in," Cassie said as she tossed her coat on a hook and grabbed an apron.

"What? No way. That would be too weird." Lexy rushed out into the front room and looked out the window to find the other baker busy behind her display case. Just as she was about to look away, a man came from the back room and Lexy noticed binoculars hanging around his neck.

"Who's that guy?" Cassie had come to stand beside her at the window.

"I don't know. Maybe her brother?"

"He has binoculars," Cassie pointed out.

"I see that, but why would they be studying us with binoculars? He's probably just bird watching or something."

Cassie raised a brow at Lexy. "Okay, if that's what you want to think, but *I* think they're scoping this place out. You said yourself that time was running short and they'd need to get into the sewer tunnels, and if Caraleigh saw the blueprints, she knows there's access through this bakery."

"True." Lexy frowned out the window. "The question is, just how far will she go to get it?"

***

Lexy and Cassie spent the rest of the day baking up fresh pastries for the bakery. The lack of customers during the week had created a glut of two-day-old baked goods, which Lexy packed up to donate to the soup kitchen. She didn't sell anything older than one day in the store, but the desserts were still good and there was no reason why someone couldn't enjoy them.

Lexy's heart swelled as she breathed in the sweet smell of cinnamon, sugar and almond. The results of the latest rendition of her scone recipe sat in rows cooling on the counter, wisps of steam rising up from their browned tops.

She felt grateful there had been a steady stream of customers today. By comparison, *The Brew and Bake* had been empty and Lexy had glanced over to catch Caraleigh looking back at her more than once. She just didn't know if the woman was looking to see how many customers she had, or trying to figure out how to get into the basement.

The jangling bell in the front signaled the departure of the latest customer Cassie had been waiting on.

Cassie breezed into the kitchen. "Oh, you added almond? Those smell so good. Can I try a little piece of one?"

"Sure." Lexy sliced into one of the scones and a gasp of steam escaped. It was still quite warm, but she managed to extract a piece, even though it fell apart on the plate. "It's not pretty, but I'm sure it will still taste good."

Cassie dug in. "Yum ... It does! This is the best one yet. You've *got* to use this recipe for the contest tomorrow."

"I don't have much choice," Lexy said. "There's no time for me to come up with any more variations."

"No need," Cassie said, shoveling the last of the crumbs into her mouth. "This one is perfection."

"Thanks," Lexy said. "I guess we might as well shut down early today. Most of the town will be at the parade practice and the evening festivities, so I don't think we'll get any business anyway ... plus the ladies are intent on exploring the sewer tunnels tonight and the sooner we get started the better."

Cassie laughed. "You couldn't persuade them not to go in there?"

"Honestly, I didn't try very hard. Not after we figured out what's really going on with *The Brew and Bake.* If our theory is true, then the sooner we find that money, the sooner Caraleigh will be out of our hair."

Cassie nodded. Lexy had told her how Caraleigh had signed out the sewer blueprints and Nans' theory of why she'd opened the bakery in the first place. "Just be careful. If she finds out what you're up to, there's no telling what she might do."

Lexy's stomach twisted. Cassie was right. Caraleigh and her brother had already gone to a lot of trouble and might resort to anything to get the treasure, but the way she saw it, she didn't have much of a choice.

The bell over the front door jingled.

"Oh, that's probably Nans." Lexy gingerly placed some of the scones on a tray, trying not to burn her fingertips. "I'll have the ladies taste-test these fresh out of the oven."

Nans, Ruth, Ida and Helen stood in the front room of the bakery looking ready for action. Their jackets hung open to reveal the same grungy paint-splattered tee-shirts they'd worn the night before.

"Good grief Lexy, we don't have time to eat," Nans said eyeing the tray Lexy held in her hand.

Lexy's heart sank. "You don't? I was hoping you'd try out my latest recipe."

"Oh, I'm so sorry dear. Of course we have time for that." Nans looked truly sorry and Lexy's demeanor brightened as she placed the scones onto paper plates.

The four ladies grabbed the plates, shoveling the scones into their mouths without even bothering to sit down.

Lexy glanced over at *The Brew and Bake* her heart skipping when she caught the other baker watching them. Caraleigh looked away quickly and busied herself with something in the bakery case.

"Mmm ... this is the best one so far," Ruth said.

"I agree," Nans added.

"Yep, it's a winner." Ida lifted the plate to her mouth and tapped the crumbs in.

"It's perfect," Helen said. "Now, let's get over to Victor's and get a key before he closes his shop."

Lexy frowned at Nans. "Are you sure you even tasted it? You scarfed them down pretty quickly."

"Yes, it truly was delicious." Nans licked the sugar that had dotted the top of the scone from her fingers and waved Lexy toward the door.

"Now remember, don't let on *why* we want the key. We don't want him to know about the door in the basement so he doesn't try to tag along," Ida said.

"What are you going to tell him?" Lexy asked.

"We're going to tell him we need it for an old trunk Helen bought at a yard sale," Nans said.

"He'll do anything to help Helen," Ida teased.

"Oh shush!" Helen swatted at her as they made their way out the door.

"Cassie, I'm going to close up out here. You can head on home ... I'll lock the front door," Lexy yelled over her shoulder as she turned out the lights, flipped the sign to "Closed" and locked the door.

She followed the ladies to Victor's shop, whose door was about thirty feet down the sidewalk. Sneaking a glance at *The Brew and Bake* as she walked, she caught Caraleigh watching them and uneasiness settled on her like a prickly wool blanket, causing her to wonder if going into the sewer tunnels was such a smart idea after all.

Chapter Fourteen

Nans ripped open the door to Victor's shop and Lexy followed the four older women in.

The shop was crammed full of old furniture and display cases with sparkling cut crystal, green and pink Depression glass, and hand painted porcelain. Vases, clocks and statues could be seen everywhere—no surface was left unadorned.

"Hi ladies. Welcome!" Lexy turned to see Victor standing behind a massive oak counter, his face lit with a welcoming smile.

"Hi, Victor." Ida made a show of looking around. "So, this is your shop? It's very nice."

"Thank you. Did you ladies just come for a social visit, or did you come to invite me on an adventure?" Victor asked hopefully.

"Actually we're here to buy something," Nans said.

"Yes, we were wondering if you had any big skeleton keys," Ruth added.

"Skeleton keys?" Victor narrowed his eyes at them. "Whatever would you need a skeleton key for?"

"Helen bought a big old trunk at a yard sale and it's locked," Nans said. "The lock takes a skeleton key."

Victor pressed his lips together. He turned in a semi-circle looking at the wall, frowned and then bent down behind the counter coming up with an iron ring about eight inches in diameter that held a collection of several skeleton keys in various shapes and sizes.

"Do you think one of these would do?" The keys tinkled together as he held the ring out to Helen.

Ida, Ruth and Nans rushed over to squint at the keys along with Helen. After a few seconds, Nans nodded.

"I think one of these two here might work." She pointed to two of the larger keys.

"How much for those?" Helen started to open her giant purse, but Victor held his hand up.

"Oh no. Just take the whole ring. You never know which key is going to fit—it's so hard to tell." He smiled at Helen. "When you find the one that fits, just bring the rest of them back. The key is on me."

"Oh well, thank you." Helen blushed.

"You're welcome." Victor leaned on the counter. "Say, did you ladies ever get into those sewer tunnels?"

"Oh no." Nans feigned disgust. "They would be so dirty."

"And dangerous," Ruth added.

"We were never going to actually go in there," Ida said. "We were just doing research ... like we said."

"Hmm ..." Victor scrunched his face up. "What were those noises I heard over there last night, then? I thought maybe you ladies were tearing up the cellar trying to get in."

Lexy's stomach lurched. "You were here last night in your shop?"

"Yep, heard a lot of banging and crashing." The orange cat jumped up on the counter in front of Victor and he scratched him behind the ears. "Scared poor Icharus here almost to death."

Nans, Ruth, Ida and Helen all wore deer-in-the-headlights looks. It was unusual for them not to be able to come up with a convincing lie to cover their tracks, so Lexy stepped in.

"Oh, I know what that was. I have a new commercial grade mixer I was trying out. The dough got all clumped up on one side and the darn thing got off kilter and started banging on the wall and making all kinds of ruckus. It took me quite a while to get it working properly."

"Is that so," Victor said warily. "Huh, well, it sure did sound like it was coming from down below."

"Nope." Lexy turned and ushered the ladies toward the door. "It was right in my kitchen."

"Oh, okay. Well, come back soon!" Victor yelled after them as they escaped out the door.

"Phew," Nans said. "Thanks for getting us out of that one, Lexy. I was stuck for words!"

"Unusual for you," Ida added causing the others to laugh as they stopped in front of *The Cup and Cake*.

Lexy unlocked the door, glancing again across the street and noticing *The Brew and Bake* was also dark with the "Closed" sign facing out. She held the door open for the ladies and then slipped in behind them, locking the door after her.

It was late afternoon and the sun cast slits of light through the window. Nans stood in the middle of the bakery, her green eyes gleaming with excitement. She rubbed her hands together.

"Okay girls," she said, a smile lighting her face. "Time to get to work."

Chapter Fifteen

The ladies raced for the basement door, their over-sized purses dangling from their arms.

"You can leave your purses in the bakery ... the door is locked," Lexy called after them as she sprinted to catch up.

"Oh no, we'll bring them," Nans yelled over her shoulder, taking the stairs two at a time. "We carry a lot of useful things in here and you never know what we might need."

Lexy shrugged and followed, listening to the keys jangle as Helen ran down the stairs with the ring in her hand.

By the time she reached the bottom of the stairs, the four ladies were already over at the door, picking out a key from the large ring.

"I think it's this one." Nans pointed to the largest key on the ring and Helen separated it, then shoved it into the lock. She pushed, wriggled and twisted, but the key did not turn.

"Try another one," Ruth said.

Helen picked another large key and tried it, but it didn't work either.

"Oh boy," Ida said. "What if none of these keys work?"

Nans pressed her lips together and then her face lit up. She pointed to the duffel bag full of tools they'd left on the floor the night before. "Why, that's no problem. We'll just use the hacksaw and cut the door up!"

"Whoa there." Lexy held her hands up. Somehow, having a big gaping hole in the basement of her bakery, leading to the sewer, didn't seem like a good idea. "Let's try all the keys first and then if we can't get one to work we'll talk about what to do next."

"Okay, okay. Don't get your panties in a bunch." Helen waved her hand at Lexy and then picked out another key. She shoved it into the lock, jiggled it, and turned.

Click.

Lexy sucked in a breath as the door swung open revealing pitch-black darkness.

Nans reached into her purse pulling out a small flashlight, which she switched on and aimed into the space behind the door. The thin beam of light illuminated a concrete tunnel, the sides spotted with something green and slimy.

Helen shrugged and stepped inside. Ruth, Ida and Nans followed.

Lexy could hear the slow drip of water from somewhere inside the tunnel, which had a dank, watery smell like the ocean flats at low tide. Her stomach clenched as she stepped through the doorway leaving the relative safety of the basement behind to enter the unknown water logged world of the old underground sewer system.

The tunnel section from Lexy's basement angled downhill for about twenty feet, then met up with another, bigger tunnel, which Lexy assumed was the main sewer conduit.

"Which way do we go?" Helen dug a flashlight, a bit larger than Nans', out of her purse and aimed the beam to the right illuminating a dark tunnel passage.

On the other side of Lexy, Nans' flashlight illuminated another long passage to the left.

"Beats me," Nans said. "If we're under the street in front of the bakery, then this way heads toward downtown."

Nans gestured with her flashlight into the tunnel on the left.

"And this way," Helen waved her flashlight toward the right, "leads toward the river."

"I vote we head toward downtown," Ida said.

"I second that," Ruth added.

"Sounds good to me." Helen shrugged, swinging the beam of her flashlight in the other direction.

The ladies took off down the tunnel slowly with Nans and Helen shining their flashlights in front of them and to the sides to illuminate the surroundings.

Lexy hadn't put much thought into what the sewer system looked like inside, but now she was getting a firsthand view. It consisted of giant concrete tubes that acted as tunnels. They were about seven feet in diameter—big enough to stand up in, but small enough to make you feel slightly claustrophobic.

The insides of the tunnels were damp. Shallow puddles of water dotted the bottom. The sides oozed with something wet. Lexy noticed chunks of concrete crumbling here and there and remembered Jack's warning about the old sewers being likely to cave in.

"Jack was right about these old tunnels being in disrepair," Lexy said. "It looks like big chunks could come lose at any time, so be careful."

Nans swung her beam of light around the edges. "Yes, I see that. Step lightly, girls."

They continued forward a few more yards until Nans suddenly stopped short, causing Lexy to skid on something slimy and bump into Ruth who turned around and gave her a dirty look.

Nans had turned to face the side of the tunnel, her flashlight pointing straight in front of her. "Girls, I think our theory was correct."

Lexy craned her neck to look around Ruth whose body blocked her view as the four ladies huddled together in front of whatever Nans had found. Lexy stood on her tiptoes, so she could look above Ruth's head, her heart skipping when she saw Nans had discovered a small room ... and it wasn't empty.

There was an opening in the cement sides of the tunnel, and a cave-like room had been carved into the earth beyond. The room measured about ten feet square and was set about two feet above the ground level of the sewer pipe. Lexy assumed that must be above the water line, which would allow the room to remain dry.

The beam of Nans' flashlight illuminated a pile of faded, dirty fabric. The room also contained an old chair, some papers and a few pallets.

Nans hopped up into the room and started poking through the debris. "Maybe the money is in here," she said excitedly.

"I think if a million dollars was stacked up in there, it would be obvious," Ida replied.

"Yeah, looks like nothing but old clothes," Ruth added.

Nans turned to them. "But this proves our theory ... someone *was* down here."

"Probably just vagrants," Ruth said.

Nans shook her head. "No. Look at the hat. It's from the 1940s."

Nans shined her light on something that lay in the corner. Even in its dilapidated state, Lexy could see it had the same shape and style as the hats they'd seen in the 1948 newspaper ad.

Lexy heard a muted *bang* and felt a vibration on the tunnel floor. Out of the corner of her eye, she saw a piece of concrete crumbling loose from the side of the tunnel.

"Look out!" She pushed Ruth aside just before the piece of concrete smashed to bits on the floor.

"Oh my," Ruth looked down at the bits of rock and dust. "Thanks Lexy. That would have hurt."

"You're welcome. What was that noise?"

"Noise?" Ruth's brows knit together.

"Yeah, didn't you hear a noise and feel the floor shaking before the cement fell?"

Ruth raised her brows at the other ladies who all shook their heads.

"I didn't hear anything," Nans said. "But we're right under the street. I bet a bus going by could cause a noise and vibration."

Lexy chewed on her bottom lip, glancing back down the tunnel uncertainly. "I suppose so, but I thought it came from back there."

"Well, we don't have time to investigate that now." Nans came out of the room back into the tunnel. "I feel we're hot on the trail of the money."

Nans proceeded up the tunnel, a little faster this time. Lexy brought up the rear, her stomach tight with anxiety as she kept her eye on the ceiling of the tunnel waiting for another chunk of concrete to fall.

Lexy wasn't paying attention to where she was going and suddenly she stepped on something soft and squishy. A small furry body ran across her foot and she let out a screech that echoed loudly down the tunnel.

The four ladies swung around to look at her, their faces etched with concern.

"What happened?'

"Are you okay?"

Lexy hopped around on one foot, her heart thudding in her chest. "Yes. But I think a rat ran across my foot!"

"Eww." Helen and Nans both made faces of disgust and trained their flashlights on the floor of the tunnel.

"I don't see any rats," Helen said.

"Me either." Nans waved her flashlight around to expose every nook and cranny of the floor.

"I tell you, something ran across my foot," Lexy said.

"Well, there's nothing here now." Nans turned to face forward. "Let's keep going."

They fell in step behind Nans. Lexy kept an eye on the tunnel behind her. Did she hear something back there? She strained her ears, but couldn't pick out anything except the sound of dripping water. It had sounded like footsteps. She hoped it wasn't more rats.

A few yards up, they came to an intersection. The main sewer tunnel continued ahead, but a smaller tunnel branched off to the right.

"Which way?" Nans shined her flashlight down one tunnel, then the other.

"I say we take the cutoff," Ida said. "If I was gonna hide stolen bank robbery money, I'd hide it down one of the side tunnels as opposed to in the main tunnel."

"Good thinking." Nans started down the tunnel off to the side.

"Wait a minute!" Helen said causing everyone to stop. "We should mark the path, so we can find our way out. This place is like a maze down here and if we take too many turns ... well, we could get lost in here and end up as skeletons just like Midas Mulcahey."

She swung her arm in front of her and snapped open her purse.

"Let's see... What do I have in here we could use?" She motioned for Ruth to hold the items as she plucked them from her purse. "Masking tape, scissors, breath mints, a scone wrapped in a napkin, a lighter ... oh here's something—lipstick. We can make a mark on the side of the tunnel so we'll know which direction to go in when we come back."

"Good idea," Nans said.

Helen sprinted to the section where the side tunnel cut off from the main one and made a mark, then sprinted back and opened her purse so Ruth could dump the items she'd been holding inside.

Okay, let's keep moving." Helen snapped her purse shut and they continued down the side tunnel. After a few feet, Lexy heard a crunch then saw Nans jump back and point her flashlight at the ground in front of her.

Ruth, who had been right behind Nans, gasped.

"Holy bone fragments," Ida said. "How many skeletons are down here?"

Lexy looked at the floor in front of Nans where the bones of a full skeleton lay.

"This one has its head," Helen said. "So it's not the rest of Midas."

"I wonder who he is?" Ruth mused.

"I think you mean *she*." Lexy pointed to the wrist, which still wore a cluster of bangles.

Nans bent down. "Well, I'll be. Looks like Midas might have had female company down here."

Ruth crouched at the head, turning it slightly.

"And looks like she met the same fate," she said pointing to a hole in the side of the skull.

"She must have been shot right here and Midas was shot further down in the main tunnel." Helen glanced back at the main tunnel. "That's why she's intact. Her body is in the offshoot here where the water doesn't rush through, so her bones didn't get washed down like Midas' did."

"So you think she was shot along with Midas?" Ruth raised a brow at Helen.

"That makes the most sense." Helen bent down to inspect her bracelets. "These look like bangles from the 1940s era. They're made from that old plastic—Bakelite. It's very collectible today."

Lexy could see the twinkle in Nans' eye as she aimed the beam of her flashlight into the dark tunnel.

"This is a good sign. I feel like we're getting closer." Nans practically skipped down the tunnel she was so excited.

Nans' excitement must have been contagious, because Lexy could feel a tingle of anticipation working its way through her veins. What if the money really was down here after all these years? Would they be able to solve Midas' murder? And find out who the other skeleton belonged to?

As they continued, the tunnel grew narrower. They were forced to stoop over and it looked like they'd eventually have to crawl. Lexy felt the enthusiasm draining from her.

"I don't think I want to crawl down there," she said. "And isn't it getting late? I told Jack I'd be home by supper."

"Maybe we *should* turn back," Ida said.

"But I was sure something would be down here." Nans' face fell and Lexy's heart crunched at the dejected sound in her voice.

"Maybe we can come back and explore another tunnel later," Helen said as they all turned.

"Yeah, I guess you guys are right." Nans gestured with her flashlight for them to turn around.

Out of the corner of her eye, Lexy saw the beam from Nans' flashlight glint off something on the wall.

"Wait a minute, what's that?" She grabbed the light from Nans and pointed it at the side of the tunnel. The original concrete of the tunnel had obviously been chipped away at some point and new concrete patched up in its place. The new concrete was crumbling away on the edges and it looked like something was behind it ... something that glinted like gold.

"Hold on." Nans lifted the flap on her giant purse and rummaged around inside coming up with a Swiss army knife. She flipped out the blade and approached the crumbling wall. Working the blade behind a crack, she wiggled and pushed until a fist-sized chunk of concrete fell out.

Lexy held the flashlight to the hole and peered in, her stomach fluttering with excitement.

"There's something back there. It looks like a small room or hiding place ... it's hard to tell, it looks like I'm looking through a window or something."

"Let me dig out more," Nans said and stabbed at the concrete with the knife.

"I can help." Ida rushed over with her own Swiss army knife.

"Me too." Ruth attacked the concrete with a nail file.

Lexy watched as they crumbled away the concrete, revealing a door with a small window near the top. The window Lexy had looked through with the flashlight earlier.

Nans reached for the door handle and, much to Lexy's surprise, the door swung open.

Lexy's eyes widened.

Nans, Ruth, Ida and Helen gasped in unison.

They were staring at a room filled with stacks of money and gold bars.

The five of them stood silent for several heartbeats. Nans was the first to speak. "We found it! We found the money! I knew it was down here!"

Click!

Lexy whirled at the metallic sound that came from behind her, her heart jerking when she came face-to-face with the barrel of a gun. Her stomach sank when a voice spoke out from the other end of the gun.

"I knew it was down here, too, but thanks for doing all the hard work and finding it for me."

Chapter Sixteen

Lexy wrenched her eyes away from the barrel of the gun and into the cold, shark-like eyes of its owner.

Caraleigh Brewster.

"You! I knew your bakery was a scam!" Lexy said.

Caraleigh laughed. "I still got more customers than you."

Lexy simmered with anger. "Yeah, well, with your grocery store pastries, I bet none of them were repeats."

"Really? If you weren't worried, then why did you steal my ring and try to frame me?"

Lexy's brows knit together. "Steal your ring? Why do you keep saying that? We know you broke in and dropped it; there's no sense in pretending now."

Caraleigh narrowed her eyes at Lexy. "Shut up. None of that matters now, anyway."

Nans held up her hands. "Well, now I think we can come to some sort of agree—"

"Zip it, old lady," Caraleigh cut Nans off and took a menacing step forward, waving her gun at all five of them. "Get in the room."

Lexy, Nans and the other ladies backed up slowly into the money room.

"Did she call me an old lady?" Nans whispered indignantly.

"Okay, listen up. You're going to load the money onto that cart." Caraleigh gestured toward one of the old metal-wheeled wooden carts that sat on the side of the room, already partially loaded with gold bars.

"And then what?" Ida asked.

"My brother, Harvey, is right behind me and we're going to wheel this money out of here, just like we planned." Caraleigh sneered at Ida.

"And what will you do with us?" Lexy asked.

Caraleigh laughed, then looked at her gun. "Harvey's gonna help me finish you ladies off. I don't think a few more skeletons down here will be a problem."

Lexy's blood froze as she heard footsteps behind Caraleigh.

That must be Harvey coming to finish them off, she thought, but then her grim thoughts turned to a stab of surprise when a gun appeared, pointing right at Caraleigh's head.

Click.

Caraleigh's face froze in a mask of confusion. "Harvey?"

"Nope. Harvey won't be coming to help you."

Lexy's heart skipped when she recognized the voice. She craned her neck to see past Caraleigh's shoulder to verify her suspicions.

"Victor! Thank god," Nans gushed.

Victor ignored Nans, his hand snaking around to Caraleigh's gun hand. "Now give me the gun nice and slow and I won't have to hurt you."

Caraleigh's eyes darted from side to side, the gun wavering back and forth in her hand.

"I know you're thinking your brother is gonna come up behind me, but I took care of him back in the basement. He's not going to come and save you," Victor said.

"What did you to do him?" Caraleigh whirled around, and Victor, with surprising agility for a man of his age, grabbed her gun and pushed her into the room.

He stood at the doorway, a gun in each hand.

"Oh, Victor! Thank you for saving us. How did you know?" Helen rushed toward Victor only to

147

stop short, a look of confusion on her face as he aimed one of the guns at her.

"Get back!" he yelled.

"Victor ... what is going on?" Nans asked.

"I didn't come here to save you, you nosey old biddies ... I came for the loot!"

***

Lexy, Nans, Ruth, Ida and Helen stared open-mouthed at Victor.

"Hey, you're the guy who stole my ring." Caraleigh crossed her arms on her chest and narrowed her eyes at him.

Lexy swiveled her head toward Caraleigh. "What? How could he steal your ring?"

Victor chuckled. "She's right. All my pick-pocket training as a young lad paid off."

"You mean the ring they found in my bakery after the break-in?" Lexy asked.

Victor nodded. "I lifted it right off her finger when I was paying for one of those god-awful stale muffins. Then I broke into your place and planted it so it would look like Caraleigh was the one who broke in."

"But why would you do that?" Nans asked.

"I was hoping to put Blondie here in jail," Victor nodded toward Caraleigh, "so she couldn't run around looking for the money. Sorry, Lexy, nothing personal."

"You knew I was here looking for the money?" Caraleigh asked.

"Of course, you look just like *her*."

"Who?" Nans, Ruth, Ida, Helen and Lexy asked, their heads ping-ponging back and forth between Victor and Caraleigh.

"Rose Cranston," Victor said wistfully. "You *are* her granddaughter, aren't you?"

Caraleigh nodded.

"Rose Cranston ... that sounds familiar," Ida's brows knit together.

"She used to run with Midas Mulcahey!" Ruth exclaimed.

Nans turned to Caraleigh. "So you knew about the money being here all along and that's why you opened the bakery across the street?"

Caraleigh nodded. "My grandmother said the money was down here somewhere. She'd made several attempts to find it, herself."

"Wait a minute," Lexy said. "That doesn't make much sense. Why didn't she just think

Midas took off with the money like everyone else?"

"She knew he didn't take off with it ... because she's the one who killed him."

"Oh well, I see you planned to follow in her footsteps," Ida snorted.

"Yeah, your grandma and Midas were pretty tight, but what Rose didn't know was that Midas was fooling around with a pretty little redhead named Scarlet on the side," Victor said.

Ruth gasped. "The other skeleton!"

"I always wondered what would happen if she found out ... Rose sure was feisty." Victor's lips curled in a smile. "I figured she took off with Midas and the money back then. Did she confess to you on her deathbed?"

Caraleigh shook her head. "No. In her diary. We read it after she passed. Apparently, she had her suspicions about Midas. She followed him down here, caught the two of them in the act and shot them. She figured Midas hid the money down here, but she never did find it."

"So once you read that in the diary, you figured you'd come and find it yourself," Nans said.

"Yep. We rented an apartment in town figuring we'd be able to find a way into the sewer system pretty easily. We didn't count on the sewer construction screwing stuff up. The blueprints showed the only entrance we could use was below *The Cup and Cake*. All we needed to do was get rid of *you* somehow." Caraleigh thrust her chin toward Lexy.

"So you sold grocery store baked goods at ridiculous prices, scammed the whole town into thinking you baked them, got a big spot on TV to draw even more people, and sabotaged my scones so that critic would give me a bad review?"

Caraleigh nodded. "Yeah ... no wait—I didn't sabotage the scones."

"That was me," Victor said proudly.

"You? Why?" Lexy couldn't help but feel betrayed by the old man who had been in the neighboring store since before she opened. All this time she'd thought he was just a nice old man ... and her friend.

"My other efforts to get rid of Caraleigh weren't working, so I figured I'd try to pit you against each other. I was hoping if Lexy got good and mad she'd have her police detective husband do something. So, I just sprinkled some cat hair in the scones one day when I came in to buy one. I distracted Lexy by dropping my cane when I was picking out a scone—already had plenty of cat hair from Icharus on my sleeve."

"So you knew about the money all this time, too?" Lexy asked.

"Knew about it? I was one of the robbers that stole it."

"You were?" Ruth wrinkled her face at him. "We read all about that robbery. I don't recall your name being mentioned."

"Oh yeah." Victor straightened, keeping the guns steadily pointed at them. "Did you hear about 'The Bomb'? That was me ... Victor Ness*baum*."

"Well, I'll be ..." Ruth said.

"Anyway," Victor continued, "Midas disappeared a couple of days after we robbed the bank. When Rose picked up and left town too, I figured the two of them took off with the money. Double-crossed the rest of us. I never even knew about his sewer hideout ... that is until I saw them dig up the skull. I knew it was Midas right away on account of the two gold teeth. That's when I put two and two together and figured the money might still be down here."

"And we led you right to it," Lexy said.

"Yes." Victor nodded his head at them. "Thanks, ladies."

"So that's why you were so interested in what we were doing," Nans said. "And all this time we thought you were sweet on Helen."

"Helen is a looker, but I'm more interested in the money. Which reminds me ... you ladies better start loading that cart before they raise the locks on the river." Victor motioned with his guns toward the cart.

"Huh? What locks?" Ida looked at Victor.

"Didn't you know?" he asked. "They do it in the years when there's been excessive rainfall to lower the level of Lake Humphrey before winter. The excess water swells the river and the runoff comes through the sewer system here. Floods it right out. Hasn't happened since 1947, so it's a good thing we got in here to get the money out in time. No telling what might happen once these sewers flood." He waved his guns at them. "Now hurry!"

Everyone, including Caraleigh, started loading up the cart. Lexy didn't dare say anything, but she hoped Nans had a plan. Should they rush Victor? She was sure they could overpower him, but with two guns pointed at them, she didn't know if it was wise to make a move toward him.

Lexy hefted the last brick of gold onto the cart and glanced sideways at Nans, her spirits sinking when she saw the worry on her grandmother's face.

"Now bring the cart here. Just you, Helen … the rest of you stay back," Victor commanded.

Helen wheeled the cart over to him.

"Drop the handle and get back," Victor said.

Helen did as asked. Victor picked up the handle and wheeled the cart out into the tunnel.

"Well, ladies, this has been fun, but now it's time to say good-bye." Victor stuffed one of the guns in his belt and grabbed the door.

"Wait. You're not going to leave us in here?" Ruth's voice was edged with panic.

"I'm afraid I must," Victor said.

"But the water's coming." Caraleigh pointed to the bottom of the tunnel, which now had a shallow, but steady stream of water running down it. "We'll drown."

"Yes. It's so sad. But I can't leave any witnesses to tell that I made off with this money now, can I?"

And with that, Victor slammed the door shut and clicked the lock into place.

Chapter Seventeen

The six of them ran to the door, their fists thudding hollowly on the solid wood.

"Hello!"

"Help!"

"Let us out!"

After several minutes, it became obvious they were wasting their energy, so they stopped yelling and banging. Lexy collapsed with her back against the door.

"We need a plan," she said.

"Don't you have one?" Nans asked.

"No, I thought you might have one."

"No."

"I know!" Ida reached in her purse. "We'll use our cell phones to call for help."

She pulled out her phone and pressed a few buttons, then held it to her ear.

After a few seconds, her brow creased.

She shook the phone and put it back to her ear.

A few more seconds and her brow creased even further.

"What the heck?" She pulled the phone away and looked at it. "Darn ... no signal!"

She walked to the corner of the room. "Maybe over here ..."

"It's no use," Ruth said. "We're underground ... the cell phone tower signals don't come in down here."

Lexy puffed out her cheeks, her heart sinking as she felt the cold water seeping under the door and soaking her shoes.

"Well, we better hurry and come up with a plan, then." She pointed to the floor. "The water is already rising."

"Yeah, you people better come up with a plan." Caraleigh glared at them with her hands fisted on her hips.

"Who are you to demand a plan?" Nans asked. "A few minutes ago you were going to shoot us!"

"Well, I wasn't going to do the actual shooting." Caraleigh looked repentant. "My brother was."

"Still, I don't think we'll be including you in our plan," Lexy said.

"Why not?" Caraleigh whined. "We're in this together now."

Lexy's brows mashed together. She couldn't believe the nerve of the woman. She took two large strides, getting right in Caraleigh's face.

"Let's get this straight." Lexy spat out the words. "We are not, and never will be, in *anything* together!"

Caraleigh straightened her spine and glared down at Lexy.

"Don't be a sore loser just because my bakery did better than yours," she said poking Lexy in the breastbone with her index finger.

The anger that had been simmering inside Lexy bubbled over. "You're nothing but a scammer. I bet you never baked even one thing in your life!"

Lexy pushed Caraleigh's shoulder. The other woman stumbled backward, crashing into the wall with the force of Lexy's anger, causing a large chunk of concrete to come loose from the top of the wall. Lexy watched in horror as the chunk tumbled down, bonking Caraleigh on the head. Caraleigh's face registered an instant of surprise, right before her eyes rolled back in their sockets and she crumpled to the floor.

Ida clapped her hands. "Yay, Lexy. You got rid of her!"

Lexy looked down at Caraleigh, her stomach twisting with anxiety. If by "getting rid of her" Ida meant she'd killed her, she certainly hoped not. It was true she didn't like the Caraleigh, but her dislike wasn't enough to go to jail for her death.

Nans squatted beside Caraleigh and picked up her wrist, feeling for a pulse.

"She's not dead, is she?" Lexy asked hopefully.

"No," Nans said, standing and brushing off her pants. "Just knocked out."

Lexy breathed a sigh of relief. "Good. I mean I know I pushed her kind of hard ... maybe too hard, but I don't want to go to jail for murder."

"I wouldn't say you pushed her too hard," Ruth said. "I'd say you pushed her just right."

"Huh?" Lexy turned to see Ruth pointing at where the concrete had come loose. Behind it, there should have been more concrete or dirt. But instead, Lexy saw a hollow darkness indicating a space behind the wall.

"Is that what I think it is?" Nans asked.

"It looks like a space," Ruth answered.

"Maybe another room," Ida said.

"Or another tunnel and a way out," Lexy suggested.

The ladies reached into their purses and dug out their Swiss army knives and nail files, then shoved Caraleigh's unconscious body out of the way and got to work on the concrete. When the hole was big enough to look through, Nans jumped up on the empty cart that had been left in the room and shoved her flashlight into the dark hole.

"It's more tunnels!"

She hopped back down and the ladies attacked the wall with renewed vigor. Lexy spotted a thick board in the corner and helped hasten the pace by using it to bang on the wall, thus causing more cracks in the old concrete.

After almost an hour of furious work, the hole was big enough for them to walk through.

"Let's go!" Ida grabbed her purse and scurried through the hole.

"What about her?" Nans pointed to Caraleigh.

"Let's just leave her," Ruth said. "She was going to shoot us and leave *us* here."

Nans gave Ruth *the look*. "We can't just leave her. The water is rising and she'll drown. We'll have to take her with us."

"How are we going to do that?" Ida's brows knit together. "Carry her?"

Nans sighed and looked around, her eyes coming to rest on the empty cart.

"We'll wheel her on the cart!" Nans said. "Helen, get out your duct tape. We'll tie her up and tape her to the cart. That way she can't cause trouble when she wakes up and we'll be able to deliver her to the police."

"That's a great idea," Helen said, digging in her purse. "We'll have solved the mystery of the skull, recovered the money stolen in the bank robbery *and* be handing over a criminal."

"That should get us a write-up in the Police Gazette for sure," Ruth said as the ladies got busy securing Caraleigh's wrists and ankles before loading her onto the cart.

"Okay, now help me get this cart out into the tunnel." Lexy lifted one end of the cart. Ruth and Helen lifted the other and they climbed over the pile of crumbled concrete, lowering the cart to the ground on the other side of the tunnel wall.

"The floor here is pretty dry. I guess the water hasn't made it this far," Lexy said.

Nans aimed the beam of her flashlight down one tunnel and then the other. There was nothing to indicate where they were or which way they should go.

"So which way do we go?" Ida asked.

Lexy felt a chill run up her spine. She could hear running water near them. How much time did they have before the tunnels filled up?

"I'm not sure," Lexy said. "But we better pick one and move forward quickly while we still have the chance."

Chapter Eighteen

"This direction is parallel to the offshoot tunnel we found the money room in," Nans said pointing straight ahead of her. "So if we go this way, I think it might intersect with the main tunnel."

"Sounds good to me," Lexy said.

They started in that direction with Lexy bringing up the rear, tugging the cart with Caraleigh strapped on it.

A few minutes later, they were at the intersection. Lexy looked at the larger tunnel, a shiver running up her spine as she noticed the water level had increased to about an inch deep.

"This must be the main tunnel." Nans aimed the beam of her flashlight to the right and then to the left.

"You mean the same one we walked down to get here?" Ruth asked.

Nans nodded.

"So, if we go to the left, we'll pass the intersection where we found the room with the money?" Ida shaded her eyes and squinted to the left as if that would help her see further into the darkness.

"Right," Nans answered. "And to the right takes us further downtown."

Helen stood in the opening, looking first right, then left. "I vote we go back the way we came. Then we can escape out the doorway in Lexy's basement."

Ruth nodded. "I agree. It's the only sure thing."

"Well, it's not really a sure thing," Lexy said. "Victor might have locked the door behind him and if he put that plank back in, we'll never get through it."

Ida's forehead creased. "But why would he do that? He thinks we're locked up in the money room. He'd have no reason to take that precaution. I vote we check it out."

"That does seem like the most logical course of action. The only other way out is the manhole cover in the center of town, and we have no idea which sewer route to take to get there." Nans turned, shining her flashlight on the group. "Are we all in?"

Lexy and the others murmured their agreement. Even Caraleigh let out a shallow groan from the cart.

As they turned to the left and sloshed into the tunnel, Lexy felt her heart squeezing in her chest. She wondered how fast the water would rise and what would happen if they got to the entryway into her basement and found the door locked. Would the water be so high by then it would block off any other route to an exit? The manhole cover in the center of town was the only other way out and, even if they could figure out how to get there, they wouldn't be able to open the cover.

"Oh look, here's the lipstick mark I made!" Helen aimed the beam of her flashlight toward the side of the tunnel where a bright red arrow marked the intersection with the tunnel they'd taken earlier.

"Good, then we *are* on the right trail." Nans' voice was edged with excitement. She picked up the pace, leading them further into the tunnel. Lexy trailed along, the last one in line.

She glanced back at the cart where Caraleigh lay, still out like a light.

Must be nice, she thought. The cart seemed to grow heavier with each step and her shoulder burned from the strain. If she wasn't faced with drowning in the cold water that was getting deeper by the minute, she might have laughed at the irony—here she was sweating it out while

Caraleigh lay on the cart sleeping blissfully as Lexy pulled her to safety.

After a few minutes, Nans slowed down, shining her light on the side of the tunnel, looking for the connector that led to Lexy's basement.

"It should be around here somewhere ..."

Lexy switched the handle of the cart to her other hand to give her arm a break and concentrated on thinking positive thoughts as she listened to the sloshing sounds their feet made while they waded through the now ankle-deep, frigid water. Her feet were starting to feel numb and heavy, like they did at the beach when the ocean temperature was in the 50s—except she suspected this water was much colder. Her heart pinched as she thought of Nans and the others— they were much older than she was, how much of this could they take?

"There it is!" Ruth pointed to something up ahead. They sloshed up to the opening and turned into the tunnel.

The short tunnel angled uphill so, thankfully, the water level dropped off quickly. Lexy now realized the buildings had been built higher than the sewer with the access tunnels, so any flooding wouldn't reach into the basement. Of course, the uphill angle made the cart even heavier, but Lexy navigated it with a burst of energy—a few more seconds and they'd be free!

Or trapped.

Nans' flashlight cast sinister shadows on the wooden door ... it was closed.

"It might not be locked," Ruth ventured.

"Right." Lexy dropped the handle of the cart and she and Nans pushed against the door.

"It opens inward, so pushing should work." Nans' voice held a tremor of uncertainty. "Maybe it's just stuck."

"Back up," Lexy commanded. She took several steps backwards then launched herself at the door, butting into it forcefully with the side of her body.

Pain exploded in her shoulder as it met the unyielding mass of the door with a dull thud. She backed up and tried again.

Did she feel the door budge just a little?

She tried again.

And again.

But the door didn't open. It was locked, probably secured with the thick piece of wood they'd removed when they opened it. *Victor had covered all his bases*, Lexy thought as she gave in to the sinking feeling they were trapped inside the sewer with nowhere to go.

"It's no use," she said, her voice cracking. Tears stung the backs of her eyes. She turned to Nans. "We're trapped."

"Nonsense!" Nans said. "*The Ladies Detective Club* does not admit defeat. There has to be another way!"

Lexy felt drained from the exertion of ramming the door. Her heartbeat drummed in her ears keeping time with her pounding headache.

"I hope there is another way," she said, massaging her temple. "Too bad I can't think with this pounding going on in my head."

"Wait a minute." Nans tilted her head. "You hear that too?"

"Yeah. You mean it's not just my head aching?"

"No, I hear it too," Ruth said.

"And me," Ida added.

Nans cocked her ear toward the main tunnel and her face lit up.

"I think I know how we can get out of here!"

Chapter Nineteen

Nans ran back into the main tunnel, the water splashing over her sensible old-lady shoes. Ruth, Ida and Helen followed with Lexy and the cart bringing up the rear.

"Mona, wait up!" Ida yelled after Nans as she waded into the tunnel.

"Can't! We have to hurry!" Nans shot back over her shoulder.

"At least tell us where we're going," Ruth said.

"Do you hear that drumbeat?" Nans asked.

"Yeees." Ida drew out the word.

"Well, that's not a migraine starting ... it's the drums from the rehearsal parade," Nans said. "You know—when they do a practice run of the entire route to make sure everything will go off without a hitch during the real parade tomorrow?"

"Yeah, so?" Helen slowed down a bit, flashing her light at the sides of the tunnel.

"Yeah, so what?" Caraleigh piped up from the cart.

Nans stopped and turned to look at them.

"Don't you guys know what that means?" she asked in an exasperated tone.

"No," Caraleigh said meekly.

"If we can follow the sounds of the parade, it will lead us straight to the center of town ..." Nans' voice drifted off as she cocked her ear toward the ceiling, apparently listening for the parade.

"And right to the manhole cover!" Ruth added.

"I think we *are* on the right track to head downtown, because we're passing the lipstick mark I made when we went into the tunnel where we found the money room." Helen pointed to the red arrow scrawled in lipstick on the wall at the juncture of two tunnels.

"Oh, by the way." Caraleigh's voice drifted up from the cart. "Thanks for making that lipstick mark. I might never have found you or the room full of money otherwise. Although in retrospect, I might have been better off if I hadn't."

Helen stared at Caraleigh. "You mean to say if I hadn't left that mark, we might not be in this predicament?"

Caraleigh shrugged as much as she could, seeing as she was bound up with duct tape. "It's hard to say."

"We don't have time for this," Nans said. "Let's go ... I hear parade noises up ahead."

"I think you guys can unstrap me from this cart," Caraleigh said. "It's not like I'm going to run away."

"Yeah right," Lexy snorted.

"It will be a lot easier on you instead of having to drag me around." Caraleigh wiggled on the cart as if to illustrate her point.

"Cut it out or I'll leave *you* tied up and the cart here," Lexy said as she struggled to drag the weaving cart through the watery tunnel.

"You wouldn't dare ... that would be sentencing me to death!"

"I still don't get why you went to all the trouble of opening a bakery when you simply could have broken into mine just like you did last night," Lexy said.

"We figured we'd need time to explore the sewers and find the money," Caraleigh explained. "If we broke in while you were still operating a business there, the break-in would be discovered the next morning when you came to open up. If we didn't find the money on the first try, we didn't know if we'd be able to break in again, so the plan was to drive you out of business and then rent the space ourselves. Then we'd have as long as we wanted to look around down here for the money."

"So why did you break in last night, then?" Helen asked.

"We found out about the sewer project cutting off the access and the locks being opened. We knew if the sewers flooded, it could wash the money away so we figured it was our last chance. I saw you leave by the front door and thought you'd gone home." Caraleigh's voice ended in a sob. "It was all Harvey's idea ... I hope that old man didn't hurt him. I just have to get out of here and make sure he's okay."

"Shhh ..." Nans hissed at them. "Will you two be quiet? I need to listen for the parade."

Nans cocked her ear toward the ceiling again and Lexy, Ruth, Ida and Helen followed suit. Lexy could just faintly hear drum beats to the left ... and the sound of rushing water to the right.

"I think it's over there." Helen pointed to the left.

"Yes, I hear it too," Nans said. "But how do we get there?"

"There's got to be a connecting tunnel." Ida sloshed ahead. "Helen, come up here with that flashlight."

"I can make a lot of ruckus if you don't untie me, and then none of us will get out of here."

Caraleigh started singing, an ungodly wail of a tune.

Lexy, Ruth and Nans put their hands on their ears.

"Stop it, that sounds awful," Ruth yelled.

"And I can make it real hard to maneuver in here too," Caraleigh wiggled on the cart, sending it swaying from side to side. The more it swayed the harder she wiggled until she'd gotten quite a momentum going. The cart splashed up water onto Ruth and Lexy. Freezing cold water.

"Hey! I've had just about enough of you," Ruth said.

"Yeah, what are you going to do about it?" Caraleigh yelled.

"I'll show you what I'm going to do. I'll shut you right up with this." Ruth rummaged in her purse, coming up with a roll of duct tape and waving it threateningly at Caraleigh who continued to rock the cart and splash water.

"Things were much nicer when she was unconscious," Nans said.

"They sure were." Ruth's eyes drifted up to the side of the tunnel where a big chunk of concrete had come lose and was ready to crumble off. "I sure hope that concrete doesn't fall and knock her out again."

"What?" Caraleigh jerked her head up, the motion causing the cart to lurch sideways, smashing against the side of the tunnel and loosening the concrete chunk. Everyone watched, wide-eyed as the chunk seemed to teeter back and forth before crashing down ... right on top of Caraleigh's head.

"Oh, heck," Caraleigh said just before it knocked her out cold.

"Well, I'll be," Ruth said. "That certainly was convenient."

Nans nodded. "Ask and you shall receive."

Helen and Ida sloshed back down to them. "There's a tunnel to the left up ahead and I can hear the parade, let's get a move on!"

Lexy grabbed the cart handle and they hustled up the sewer tunnel, turning left behind Ida and Helen. Once they were a few feet into the tunnel, the parade sounds became much more distinguishable.

"I can hear it!" Lexy said.

"If this is main street, the manhole should be dead ahead." Nans took off at a sprint.

Lexy tugged on the cart. It was getting heavier. The steadily rising water was almost up to the level of the cart's platform, any higher and they'd have to do something to keep Caraleigh from drowning. Lexy's arm burned, her breath came out in shallow puffs. She didn't know how much longer she could pull the cart.

"I see it!" Nans' excited shout echoed down the tunnel giving Lexy a burst of energy. Nans stood about fifty feet away looking up. Lexy could see shafts of light filtering down from the holes in the manhole cover above.

Ruth, Ida and Helen caught up to Nans and the four of them jumped up and down, waving their arms and yelling.

"Hello!"

"Down here!"

"Yoo-hoo!"

Lexy doubted anyone above would be able to hear them over the din of the parade. She pulled the cart up to the group of women and pushed them aside.

"Hold on, I'll try and push the cover off," she yelled.

The roof of the tunnel was about seven feet tall. Metal rungs leading up to the manhole cover were embedded in the side of the tunnel. Lexy reached out and grabbed one, the cold, clammy metal chilling her hands. She hoisted herself up, putting her feet on the lower rung and climbing the other two, her wet feet slipping as she went.

She only needed to climb up a few feet before she was high enough. She put both her palms on the cover. She pushed with all her might.

It didn't budge.

She tried again.

Nothing.

"Help!" she yelled up through the holes, but she knew it was no use. No one would hear her, the parade was too loud. She crawled back down the metal rungs.

"It's no use," she said as she splashed off the last rung into the water, her heart sinking. "The parade is too loud."

"Oh dear." Helen wrung her hands. "What are we going to do?"

"I have an idea!" Nans snapped open her purse and, much to Lexy's amazement, pulled out a dental mirror.

Lexy's chest tightened as she watched Nans scramble up the metal rungs. "Be careful Nans," she said. "Why don't you let me do that?"

Nans waved her off with one hand while she thrust the dental mirror up with the other. Moving the mirror, she angled her head this way and that.

"Are you signaling an S.O.S.?" Ida asked.

"Nope." Nans wiggled the dental tool some more, then squinted up into the opening, so she could see what was happening up above in the reflection of the mirror. "Oh, there it is!"

"What?" Lexy squinted up at Nans.

"The guide dog float is coming up next!" Nans said.

"So?"

"Do you guys still have those scones in your purses?" Nans asked Ruth, Ida and Helen.

The three looked thoughtful and then opened their purses.

"I don't rightly remember," Ida said as she dug in the purse. "Oh, I do!"

She pulled out the napkin wrapped scone and held it up to Nans.

"Me too!" Ruth said.

"Here's mine." Helen held up hers.

"Give me yours, Ida." Nans reached down and took the package from Ida, opening it up and pinching off a piece of scone, which she pushed up through the small hole in the cover.

"What in the world are you doing?" Ida asked.

"Creating a ruckus so we'll get noticed." Nans pushed more bits of scone through the cover then gestured to Helen to hand up her scone, which Nans broke into bits and pushed up.

Suddenly the parade noises were drowned out by the sounds of sniffing, then a few short yips and a couple of growls. Nans shoved one more piece of scone up through the cover and the air erupted in a frenzy of barking.

"Hey, Hey. What is going on?" A voice carried down to them. Lexy noticed the parade noises had stopped, presumably due to the ruckus caused by the dogs fighting over the pieces of scone.

"Hey!" Nans yelled up at the cover.

"Is that someone down there?" She heard a voice.

"Yes, we're stuck down here ... can you get the cover off so we can get out?"

"Hold on, let me get the cop on detail," The voice said.

Lexy heard feet shuffling above and then a familiar voice. "Are you trying to tell me someone is down there, in the sewer?"

"Yes, we're down here and we've caught a criminal," Nans yelled up. "I do wish you would hurry and remove the manhole cover to let us out, though. The water in the sewer is rising. I fear I've already ruined my new orthopedic shoes."

"Wait a minute ... Mona is that you?" Lexy's heart lurched when she realized to whom the voice belonged.

"Why, yes it is ... Jack?" Nans looked at Lexy and shrugged.

"Yeah, it's me. Let me guess, you guys went down in there to investigate the murder even though I said not to, right?"

"Yes," Nans said sheepishly.

"And I'm sure Lexy is down there, too," Jack said.

Lexy grimaced, remembering Jack had told her he'd pulled a detail for the bicentennial celebration—it was just her luck he'd be the one to be stationed near the manhole.

"But we found out who the killer is *and* figured out who broke into Lexy's bakery *and* recovered the money from the 1948 bank robbery," Ida said proudly.

"Well, *almost* recovered the money," Helen added.

"What are you guys talking about?" Jack asked.

"Never mind now," Nans yelled. "Just get us out of here."

"I'll have to get the sewer guys here to lift the plate," Jack said.

Lexy heard police radio noises and then Jack saying, "Hey, you won't believe who's down here."

"Now who's he talking to?" Ruth asked.

"Baker? Are you down there?" The unmistakable voice of Watson Davies drifted down through the manhole cover and Lexy rolled her eyes.

"Yes, and you won't believe it, but we captured Caraleigh in the act."

"The baker from *The Brew and Bake*?" Davies asked.

"Yep, she really was up to no good." Lexy cast a glance at Caraleigh who lay unconscious on the cart, the water now perilously close to her face.

"So, she was the one that broke into your bakery?"

"Well, not the first time," Lexy said.

"First time? What is going on down there?"

Nans cut in. "We'll tell you when we get out. Now for Pete's sake, will you open the darn manhole cover? The water is rising and we have another criminal to catch before it's too late!"

Chapter Twenty

Lexy heard the scraping of metal on the manhole cover and the round circle slid back, revealing the glorious blue sky. Nans burst out of the hole before the cover made it all the way off.

"Are you all okay?" Lexy could hear Jack's concerned voice as she watched Ruth, Ida, and Helen line up at the metal rungs to make their escape.

"Never mind about us," Nans snapped. "We need a police car, pronto. The perp could be getting away!"

Davies face squinted at Lexy from the manhole opening. "Are you coming out, Baker?"

"Yeah, but we have to get Caraleigh out first." Lexy pointed to the cart and Davies aimed her police issue flashlight in that direction.

"Is she alive?" Davies asked.

"Yes, of course." Lexy rolled her eyes.

"Okay, I'll get the EMT's to climb down and get her, you come on up."

Lexy cast one last glance at Caraleigh before she started up the ladder. The water lapped at the top of the cart. But, what did she care? Caraleigh would have left Lexy to drown. Besides, they'd be down to get her out before the water covered her.

Lexy took a deep breath as she emerged from the hole, filling her lungs with glorious fresh air. She squinted, her eyes adjusting to the light—even though it was almost dusk, it was still so much brighter than inside the tunnel and it made her eyes hurt. She was tired and cold, but couldn't help but feel incredibly grateful they'd gotten out unscathed.

She didn't have much time to enjoy the feeling though, because a black and white police car skidded to a stop and Nans sprang into action.

"Here's the car," Nans yelled as she hustled toward it. "Come on girls!"

Nans opened the back door and hopped in. Somehow, Ruth, Ida and Helen managed to squeeze themselves in the back with her.

"Lexy get in front," Nans ordered out the window, her hand waving wildly at the front of the car. "Hurry up!"

Lexy cast an uncertain glance at Jack who shrugged, and then gestured to the car as if to say, "go ahead".

She ran for the car, hopped in the front and pulled the door to close it. She'd only succeeded in closing it halfway when it was ripped open and

Watson Davies swung inside, shoving Lexy over on the bench seat.

"To Lexy's bakery! Punch it!" Nans yelled.

The car lurched forward in a blaze of red and blue lights, the sirens blaring. As they sped off, Lexy peeked out the side window at Jack who stared back at her, his lips curled in a smile.

Was he shaking his head?

She gave him a tentative finger wave, hoping he wouldn't be mad at her for this latest escapade. He answered by blowing her a kiss and Lexy's heart soared. Surely, that was a sign he wasn't mad at her.

They squealed around the corner and Nans tapped the driver on the shoulder.

"Turn off the lights and siren," she yelled in his ear. "We don't want to warn him off if he's in there."

Davies half turned in the seat to face Nans. "Who are you taking about?"

"Victor. The man who owns the antique shop. It seems he was in on the 1948 bank robbery. He found us down in the sewer, stole the money, and left us to die."

"So that money really was still down there after all these years?" Davies asked.

"Yep, and we discovered the identity of the skull *and* who killed him," Nans said smugly.

"*And* another skeleton to boot," Ida added.

Davies lifted a brow and Nans told her how Caraleigh had found the confession in her grandmother's diary and her plan to run Lexy out of business.

"I *knew* she was up to something," Davies said.

"Okay, slow down here and park before you get to the antique store," Nans said. "We don't want to spook him."

The police car pulled to the curb and they spilled out. Nans crept up to the antique store and peeked in the window.

"I don't see anyone in there," she said.

"He's probably long gone by now," Helen answered.

"If he's smart," Ruth added.

"But we still need to go see what he did to Caraleigh's brother. He said he took care of him in Lexy's basement ... whatever that means." Nans started toward the back of the building.

Lexy glanced into Victor's antique store as she followed the group to the back.

Did she see a beam of light filtering in from an open door?

It would make sense if Victor left in a hurry. He probably left his back door open.

They came around the corner and Lexy's breath caught in her throat when she saw the back door to her shop practically hanging off the hinges.

"What the heck?" Lexy remembered the noise she'd heard when they were in the tunnel and realized it must have been Caraleigh and her brother breaking down the door.

"Looks like someone mutilated it with a sledge hammer." Davies turned to Lexy. "You know, you really should get better security back here with the way you keep getting broken into."

Lexy rushed inside. *Had anything been stolen?* She glanced into the kitchen on her way to the front room. Everything seemed to still be in its place. Luckily, no one had noticed the back door hanging open in the empty bakery and come in to help themselves.

She made her way to the back of the bakery, meeting Davies and the other police officer who were on their way to the basement.

"You stay up here until we secure the area," Davies said to her.

Lexy started outside to inspect the door. Nans, Ruth, Ida and Helen were standing just inside the back door, craning their necks toward the basement.

"Did she say to stay up here?" Ruth asked.

"I think so," Ida said. "But I want to see what's down there."

"Me too." Helen took a step toward the basement door. "We're old ladies and we don't hear so good, maybe we thought she said to come right down ..."

Ruth, Nans and Ida tittered as they inched their way toward the basement door.

Lexy couldn't help but laugh at the adventurous older ladies as she made her way outside to inspect the damage to the door.

The doorknob had been busted clean off, the steel door pocked with dents. *I'll have to buy a new one,* she thought ruefully as she stood staring at it with her arms crossed on her chest.

"Meow."

Lexy turned to see Icharus, Victor's orange tiger cat, rubbing his chin against the dumpster. Her heart pinched. Apparently, Victor had taken off and left the cat. Who would care for it now? Lexy squatted down to scratch the cat's head, wondering if Sprinkles might like a furry friend.

"Lexy—you coming?" Nans poked her head out the back door.

"In a sec." Lexy listened to the cat purr. "You poor thing, don't worry, I'll make sure you get taken care—"

Lexy's words cut off in mid-sentence, her heart jerking in her chest as a hand shot out from behind the dumpster and clamped over her wrist.

She tried to pull away, but was dragged to the other side of the dumpster instead.

"Victor!"

Jeez, the old guy is strong, Lexy thought as she tried to jerk her wrist free.

"That's right," he said and Lexy's stomach sank as she felt cold metal against the side of her head—Victor's gun. "You're gonna be my ticket out of here."

Victor shoved her toward his car, which had been hidden behind the dumpster the whole time.

"Hold it right there, Victor."

Lexy looked up to see Nans standing about twenty feet away, her hand inside her purse and her purse held out in front of her, pointed at Victor.

Victor pulled Lexy in front of him like a shield, the gun still hard against the side of her head.

"I have a gun in here and I'm not afraid to use it." Nans gestured with her purse. "I'll shoot a hole right through my purse without even thinking twice."

When did Nans start carrying a gun?

"Put it down or I'll shoot Lexy," Victor hissed.

"Let Lexy go, or I'll shoot *you*." Nans stood her ground.

"Ha! Looks like we're at a stalemate then." Victor cackled as he shuffled backwards toward the car, pulling Lexy with him and whispering to her. "I'm gonna slide into the car nice and slow and you're comin' in after me. You'll have no choice since I'll still have the gun to your head."

Lexy saw Nans' eyes widen a fraction of an inch, and then heard a muffled noise behind her. Victor must have heard the noise too, because he turned his head slightly to look over his shoulder in that direction.

Too bad he kept shuffling backward because, by the time he realized the noise was Helen, who had snuck up and crouched behind them on all fours, his legs had hit her and he was falling backwards.

Victor let go of Lexy, his arms flailing in the air as he fell.

The gun flew out of his hand and clattered on the pavement.

Lexy jumped on the gun, while Nans and Helen jumped on Victor, straddling his torso to keep him from getting away.

"What the *hell* is going on here?" Davies came around the dumpster, her gun drawn.

"Looks like we captured the bad guy for you," Helen said proudly.

Davies' brows shot up as she studied the scene in front of her. Victor lay on his back on the ground with Nans sitting on his chest and Helen on his knees. His face turned deeper shades of red as he banged his fists on the ground and mumbled expletives. The orange cat sat two feet away, licking his paws and flicking his tail.

"I guess Victor hadn't finished loading his car yet." Lexy pointed to the late model Dodge behind Victor with its trunk and backseat filled with stacks of money and bars of gold. "He grabbed me from behind the dumpster. He had a gun and planned to use me as a hostage to get away."

Lexy held the gun out to Davies, who produced a plastic bag from her pocket, holding it open for Lexy to put the gun inside.

"We heard something going on out here and came to Lexy's rescue," Nans said. "I distracted

Victor while Helen went around from the back and tripped him up."

Helen and Nans giggled at Nans' literal explanation.

"Thanks for coming to my rescue," Lexy said to the two older women, then frowned at Nans. "Since when did you start carrying a gun?"

"I didn't" Nans looked at her purse. "That whole gun in the purse thing was just a bluff."

Chapter Twenty One

"See, I *knew* you'd win first prize." Jack pecked a kiss on Lexy's nose as she fingered the silky blue ribbon she held in her hand, her chest swelling with pride.

They walked, hand in hand, through the crowd at the Brook Ridge Falls bicentennial celebration. The smell of cotton candy and popcorn spiced the crisp fall air. Lexy pinned the ribbon to her lapel, then pulled her jean jacket tight to ward off the chill.

"Luckily, that bad review from Edgar Royce in the *Sentinel* didn't put any of the judges off," Lexy said.

"That pompous ass? No one pays attention to his reviews anyway." Jack scoffed. "It probably helped you win."

"Do you see Nans and the girls?" Lexy squinted into the crowd. "She said they'd meet us here."

"Yoo-hoo! Lexy!"

Lexy turned to see Nans, Ruth, Helen, Ida and Ida's fiancé, Norm, waving to them at the edge of the crowd. The four women looked like quadruplets with their matching tan trench coats, giant patent leather purses and sensible shoes. She tugged Jack toward them.

"There you guys are. We were looking for you," Lexy said.

"Oh, we've been here for a while," Ruth answered.

"We've already picked up some of Myra Biddeford's prize-winning jam," Helen said pulling a strawberry jam-filled glass jar with a red and white checkered ribbon around it from her purse.

"And seen Miles O'Brien's fancy hens and roosters," Ida said, then leaned toward Lexy and whispered in her ear. "I think Helen's kind of sweet on Miles."

"And now we're ready to head to the beer tent," Helen added.

"Perfect. John and Cassie are supposed to meet us there," Jack said.

"I've got the map right here." Nans held out a pamphlet that showed a map of the bicentennial fairgrounds. "Now if I could just figure out how to get there."

"Where is it?" Lexy looked over Nans' shoulder at the map.

"The beer tent is here." Nans pointed to a spot on the map. "I just don't know where *we* are."

"I think we're here." Lexy leaned over and pointed, the ends of the blue ribbon fluttering on the map.

"Oh, where are my manners!" Nans exclaimed. "You won first prize with the scones?"

Lexy nodded, blushing slightly.

"Congratulations," everyone chorused as Nans squeezed Lexy into a hug.

"Thanks," Lexy said. "I'm just glad I was around to actually bake them. That was a close call in the sewer."

"Well, thankfully that Caraleigh person won't be bothering you or taking business from your bakery anymore," Nans answered.

"So, what exactly *did* happen last night?" Ruth's brow creased as she looked at Jack. "I mean how did Caraleigh and Victor find us in the sewer?"

"From the statements we got, it seems Caraleigh and her brother didn't know you had gone down to the sewer. She said she saw you leave through the front door," Jack said.

"That's right," Ruth replied. "We went to Victor's, but then we went back to Lexy's after we got the key to open the door."

"I saw her watching us," Lexy said. "She must have seen us leave and didn't realize we came back."

"Apparently, Victor was watching too," Jack continued. "Because he saw Caraleigh and Harvey break into *The Cup and Cake* through the back. He already guessed they were after the money, so he simply followed them in. His plan was to capture all of you together, but Harvey surprised him in the basement and Victor had to knock him out."

"So, Victor is going to jail?" Nans asked.

"Yep. Not only for what he did in the sewer, but also for his part in the 1948 robbery. He's just lucky he didn't kill Harvey or he'd be getting a much stiffer sentence."

"Justice has been served," Ida said. "But I'm a little peeved there was no reward for finding the stolen money."

"Sorry about that." Jack spread his hands. "That's up to the bank, not us."

"One thing still bothers me," Ruth said.

"What's that?"

"The ring Lexy found in *The Cup and Cake* after the first break in ... how did Victor steal that from Caraleigh?"

Jack laughed. "Victor was a pickpocket back in the day, so he had a whole bag full of tricks. Apparently, he had some way of slipping the ring off a person's finger without them noticing. He said he did it when he bought a muffin from her shop and they were exchanging the money."

"That confirms what he told us in the tunnel," Helen said.

"And Caraleigh and Harvey ... are *they* going to jail?" Lexy asked.

Jack's face hardened. "Unfortunately, we don't have much to charge them with. Victor interrupted their plan to take the money and leave you guys in the sewer, so all we have is some minor charges. They'll probably get off with parole because, the truth is, they never actually did anything wrong other than break into the bakery."

"So, Victor did them a big favor," Nans said.

Lexy made a face. "That hardly seems fair. Their whole bakery was a scam and they did a lot of bad things, not to mention they were going to steal all the money and leave us for dead!"

"I know." Nans rubbed Lexy's back soothingly. "Let's just be glad they'll be leaving town and we've seen the last of them."

"Oh, I don't know if you've seen the last of them," a voice behind Nans said. Lexy turned to see Watson Davies decked out in a knee-length black leather jacket over faded denim jeans and black mid-calf boots. She had something bulky inside her jacket, but Lexy didn't have time to speculate, she was more concerned about why she said they hadn't seen the last of the Brewster's.

"Why not?" Lexy wrinkled her face at Davies.

"I just came from the station and Caraleigh is pressing charges against the five of you for kidnapping and assault," Davies said.

Nans, Ruth, Ida, Helen, and Lexy exchanged open-mouthed looks.

"Are you serious?" Lexy asked.

Davies half shrugged. "Yep."

"Well, I never," Helen said.

"That sure does take the cake," Nans added. "No pun intended."

"Surely, they won't win?' Lexy asked. "Will they?"

Jack shook his head. "Of course not. They're just mad because their plans got ruined and they're trying to get revenge."

Ruth snorted. "Yeah. By now they figured they'd be sitting on top of a fortune like a couple of fat cats."

"Speaking of cats," Lexy said. "I wonder what's going to happen to Victor's cat. I saw him out by the dumpster this morning when I went in to bake the scones, but he wasn't there when I left."

"Oh, I think he'll be fine," Davies said as she opened her jacket to reveal she had been holding the orange tiger cat the whole time.

"Davies, you really do have a heart!" Nans said.

Davies shrugged. "He was there by the dumpster crying when I went over to remove the crime scene tape and I figured I could use him at my place to chase down the mice."

"Well, it's good to see someone is getting something out of this whole mess," Jack said, then turned to Nans and the ladies. "I hate to say I told you so, but I think you all can agree if you'd listened to me when I said you shouldn't go in the sewers you'd have been better off."

"Well, I don't know about that," Ida said indignantly. "I don't think the real killer of Midas

Mulcahey and the woman that was killed with him would have been uncovered, or the money from the bank robbery found."

"Yeah," Nans said, then withered a bit under Jack's piercing look. "But you were right about it being dangerous."

Nans looked back down at the map and then pointed to the left. "I think the beer tent is that way."

"So you're going to listen to me from now on, right Mona?" Jack asked.

"What?" Nans turned to look at Jack. "Oh, we'll listen. We promise to never go in the sewers again. Don't we, girls?"

"Of course," Ruth said.

"Sure thing," Ida added.

"You bet," Helen agreed.

Jack rolled his eyes, then draped his arm over Lexy's shoulders and turned in the direction Nans had pointed to earlier. "Come on then, ladies. Let's get to the beer tent. The least you can all do is to buy me a beer."

The end.

A Note From The Author

Thanks so much for reading my cozy mystery *"Scones, Skulls & Scams"*. I hope you liked reading it as much as I loved writing it. If you did, and feel inclined to leave a review over at Amazon, I really would appreciate it.

This is book eight of the Lexy Baker series, you can find the rest of the books on my website, or over at Amazon if you want to read more of Lexy's and Nans's adventures.

Also, if you like cozy mysteries, you might like my book *"Dead Wrong"* which is book one in the Blackmoore Sisters series. Set in the seaside town of Noquitt Maine, the Blackmoore sisters will take you on a journey of secrets, romance and maybe even a little magic. I have an excerpt from it at the end of this book.

This book has been through many edits with several people and even some software programs, but since nothing is infallible (even the software programs) you might catch a spelling error or mistake and, if you do, I sure would appreciate it if you let me know - you can contact me at *lee@leighanndobbs.com*.

Oh, and I love to connect with my readers so please do visit me on facebook at *http://www.facebook.com/leighanndobbsbooks*

Signup to get my newest releases at a discount and notification of contests:

http://www.leighanndobbs.com/newsletter

About The Author

Leighann Dobbs discovered her passion for writing after a twenty year career as a software engineer. She lives in New Hampshire with her husband Bruce, their trusty Chihuahua mix Mojo and beautiful rescue cat, Kitty. When she's not reading, gardening or selling antiques, she likes to write romance and cozy mystery novels and novelettes which are perfect for the busy person on the go.

Find out about her latest books and how to get discounts on them by signing up at:

http://www.leighanndobbs.com/newsletter

Connect with Leighann on Facebook and Twitter

http://facebook.com/leighanndobbsbooks
http://twitter.com/leighanndobbs

More Books By Leighann Dobbs

Lexy Baker
Cozy Mystery Series
* * *
Lexy Baker Cozy Mystery Series Boxed Set Vol 1
(Books 1-4)

Or buy the books separately:

Killer Cupcakes (Book 1)
Dying For Danish (Book 2)
Murder, Money and Marzipan (Book 3)
3 Bodies and a Biscotti (Book 4)
Brownies, Bodies & Bad Guys (Book 5)
Bake, Battle & Roll (Book 6)
Wedded Blintz (Book 7)

Blackmoore Sisters
Cozy Mystery Series
* * *
Dead Wrong
Dead & Buried
Dead Tide
Buried Secrets

Kate Diamond
Adventure/Suspense Series
* * *

Hidden Agemda

Contemporary
Romance
* * *

Sweet Escapes
Reluctant Romance

Dobbs "Fancytales"
Regency Romance Fairytales Series
* * *

Something In Red
Snow White and the Seven Rogues
Dancing On Glass
The Beast of Edenmaine
The Reluctant Princess
***

Excerpt From Dead Wrong:

Morgan Blackmoore tapped her finger lightly on the counter, her mind barely registering the low buzz of voices behind her in the crowded coffee shop as she mentally prioritized the tasks that awaited her back at her own store.

"Here you go, one yerba mate tea and a vanilla latte." Felicity rang up the purchase, as Morgan dug in the front pocket of her faded denim jeans for some cash which she traded for the two paper cups.

Inhaling the spicy aroma of the tea, she turned to leave, her long, silky black hair swinging behind her. Elbowing her way through the crowd, she headed toward the door. At this time of morning, the coffee shop was filled with locals and Morgan knew almost all of them well enough to exchange a quick greeting or nod.

Suddenly a short, stout figure appeared, blocking her path. Morgan let out a sharp breath, recognizing the figure as Prudence Littlefield.

Prudence had a long running feud with the Blackmoore's which dated back to some sort of run-in she'd had with Morgan's grandmother when they were young girls. As a result, Prudence loved to harass and berate the Blackmoore girls in public. Morgan's eyes darted around the room, looking for an escape route.

"Just who do you think you are?" Prudence demanded, her hands fisted on her hips, legs spaced shoulder width apart. Morgan noticed she was wearing her usual knee high rubber boots and an orange sunflower scarf.

Morgan's brow furrowed over her ice blue eyes as she stared at the older woman's prune like face.

"Excuse me?"

"Don't you play dumb with me Morgan Blackmoore. What kind of concoction did you give my Ed? He's been acting plumb crazy."

Morgan thought back over the previous week's customers. Ed Littlefield *had* come into her herbal remedies shop, but she'd be damned if she'd announce to the whole town what he was after.

She narrowed her eyes at Prudence. "That's between me and Ed."

Prudence's cheeks turned crimson. Her nostrils flared. "You know what *I* think," she said narrowing her eyes and leaning in toward Morgan, "I think you're a witch, just like your great-great-great-grandmother!"

Morgan felt an angry heat course through her veins. There was nothing she hated more than being called a witch. She was a Doctor of

Pharmacology with a Master Herbalist's license, not some sort of spell-casting conjurer.

The coffee shop had grown silent. Morgan could feel the crowd staring at her. She leaned forward, looking wrinkled old Prudence Littlefield straight in the eye.

"Well now, I think we know that's not true," she said, her voice barely above a whisper, "Because if I was a witch, I'd have turned you into a newt long ago."

Then she pushed her way past the old crone and fled out the coffee shop door.

***

Fiona Blackmoore stared at the amethyst crystal in front of her wondering how to work it into a pendant. On most days, she could easily figure out exactly how to cut and position the stone, but right now her brain was in a pre-caffeine fog.

Where was Morgan with her latte?

She sighed, looking at her watch. It was ten past eight, Morgan should be here by now, she thought impatiently.

Fiona looked around the small shop, *Sticks and Stones*, she shared with her sister. An old cottage that had been in the family for generations, it sat at one of the highest points in their town of Noquitt, Maine.

Turning in her chair, she looked out the back window. In between the tree trunks that made up a small patch of woods, she had a bird's eye view of the sparkling, sapphire blue Atlantic Ocean in the distance.

The cottage sat about 500 feet inland at the top of a high cliff that plunged into the Atlantic. If the woods were cleared, like the developers wanted, the view would be even better. But Fiona would have none of that, no matter how much the developers offered them, or how much they needed the money. She and her sisters would never sell the cottage.

She turned away from the window and surveyed the inside of the shop. One side was setup as an apothecary of sorts. Antique slotted shelves loaded with various herbs lined the walls. Dried weeds hung from the rafters and several mortar and pestles stood on the counter, ready for whatever herbal concoctions her sister was hired to make.

On her side sat a variety of gemologist tools and a large assortment of crystals. Three antique oak and glass jewelry cases displayed her creations. Fiona smiled as she looked at them. Since childhood she had been fascinated with rocks and gems so it was no surprise to anyone when she grew up to become a gemologist and jewelry designer, creating jewelry not only for its beauty, but also for its healing properties.

The two sisters vocations suited each other perfectly and they often worked together providing customers with crystal and herbal healing for whatever ailed them.

The jangling of the bell over the door brought her attention to the front of the shop. She breathed a sigh of relief when Morgan burst through the door, her cheeks flushed, holding two steaming paper cups.

"What's the matter?" Fiona held her hand out, accepting the drink gratefully. Peeling back the plastic tab, she inhaled the sweet vanilla scent of the latte.

"I just had a run in with Prudence Littlefield!" Morgan's eyes flashed with anger.

"Oh? I saw her walking down Shore road this morning wearing that god-awful orange sunflower scarf. What was the run-in about this time?" Fiona took the first sip of her latte, closing her eyes and waiting for the caffeine to power her blood stream. She'd had her own run-ins with Pru Littlefield and had learned to take them in stride.

"She was upset about an herbal mix I made for Ed. She called me a witch!"

"What did you make for him?"

"Just some Ginkgo, Ginseng and Horny Goat Weed ... although the latter he said was for Prudence."

Fiona's eyes grew wide. "Aren't those herbs for impotence?"

Morgan shrugged "Well, that's what he wanted."

"No wonder Prudence was mad...although you'd think just being married to her would have caused the impotence."

Morgan burst out laughing. "No kidding. I had to question his sanity when he asked me for it. I thought maybe he had a girlfriend on the side."

Fiona shook her head trying to clear the unwanted images of Ed and Prudence Littlefield together.

"Well, I wouldn't let it ruin my day. You know how *she* is."

Morgan put her tea on the counter, then turned to her apothecary shelf and picked several herbs out of the slots. "I know, but she always seems to know how to push my buttons. Especially when she calls me a witch."

Fiona grimaced. "Right, well I wish we *were* witches. Then we could just conjure up some money and not be scrambling to pay the taxes on this shop and the house."

Morgan sat in a tall chair behind the counter and proceeded to measure dried herbs into a mortar.

"I know. I saw Eli Stark in town yesterday and he was pestering me about selling the shop again."

"What did you tell him?"

"I told him we'd sell over our dead bodies." Morgan picked up a pestle and started grinding away at the herbs.

Fiona smiled. Eli Stark had been after them for almost a year to sell the small piece of land their shop sat on. He had visions of buying it, along with some adjacent lots in order to develop the area into high end condos.

Even though their parents early deaths had left Fiona, Morgan and their two other sisters property rich but cash poor the four of them agreed they would never sell. Both the small shop and the stately ocean home they lived in had been in the family for generations and they didn't want *their* generation to be the one that lost them.

The only problem was, although they owned the properties outright, the taxes were astronomical and, on their meager earnings, they were all just scraping by to make ends meet.

All the more reason to get this necklace finished so I can get paid. Thankfully, the caffeine had finally cleared the cobwebs in her head and Fiona was ready to get to work. Staring down at the amethyst, a vision of the perfect shape to cut the stone appeared in her mind. She grabbed her tools and started shaping the stone.

Fiona and Morgan were both lost in their work. They worked silently, the only sounds in the little shop being the scrape of mortar on pestle and the hum of Fiona's gem grinding tool mixed with a few melodic tweets and chirps that floated in from the open window.

Fiona didn't know how long they were working like that when the bell over the shop door chimed again. She figured it must have been an hour or two judging by the fact that the few sips left in the bottom of her latte cup had grown cold.

She smiled, looking up from her work to greet their potential customer, but the smile froze on her face when she saw who it was.

Sheriff Overton stood in the door flanked by two police officers. A toothpick jutted out of the side of Overton's mouth and judging by the looks on all three of their faces, they weren't there to buy herbs or crystals.

Fiona could almost hear her heart beating in the silence as the men stood there, adjusting their eyes to the light and getting their bearings.

"Can we help you?" Morgan asked, stopping her work to wipe her hands on a towel.

Overton's head swiveled in her direction like a hawk spying a rabbit in a field.

"That's her." He nodded to the two uniformed men who approached Morgan hesitantly. Fiona recognized one of the men as Brody Hunter, whose older brother Morgan had dated all through high school. She saw Brody look questioningly at the Sheriff.

The other man stood a head taller than Brody. Fiona noticed his dark hair and broad shoulders but her assessment of him stopped there when she saw him pulling out a pair of handcuffs.

Her heart lurched at the look of panic on her sister's face as the men advanced toward her.

"Just what is this all about?" She demanded, standing up and taking a step toward the Sheriff.

There was no love lost between the Sheriff and Fiona. They'd had a few run-ins and she thought he was an egotistical bore and probably crooked too. He ignored her question focusing his attention on Morgan. The next words out of his mouth chilled Fiona to the core.

"Morgan Blackmoore ... you're under arrest for the murder of Prudence Littlefield."

32036769R00122

Made in the USA
Lexington, KY
04 May 2014